SIEGE
OF THE
NORTHLAND

RUTH RATHBAND

Copyright © Ruth Rathband 2017

Published by Kaluta Press

First published as an ebook 2017:
ISBN 978-1-9997183-1-2

First published as a paperback 2017:
ISBN 978-1-9997183-0-5

Cover design and typesetting by Raspberry Creative Type

Part One: Awakening

Long ago in a distant land ...

1

In the northern territories of the Eastland, a small party on horseback gathered on a hilltop beneath a dull descending sky; below them, and for as far as the eye could see, a slaughter was underway of men, women and children. The crackle and roar of burning homes and flesh, accompanied by the clamour of terrified livestock and the unceasing cries of those dispensing the terror, only added to the mournful chorus of human despair that fouled the air.

Volger, breaking away from the party, urged his horse forward a few paces, his attention taken by the progress of a man being dragged by his hair up the rocky hillside by two armour-clad warriors.

"Dear God!" cried Volger, holding a red silken handkerchief before his nose. "I will never get used to this infernal smell."

The man was dumped without ceremony before Volger's horse; drawing back his black fur-rimmed hood, he leant forward to view the prisoner more closely. Volger's long, pale face and somewhat over-large jaw bore an expression of indifference as he continued to redirect the stench away from his nostrils.

"Ah, at last – I take it you are Greschwen, King of the Eastland?" He wrinkled his offended nose. "Dear me, you seem to have lost your crown."

Greschwen's lips quivered, parting slightly, but no words came.

"So," Volger continued, "what is your pleasure? Will you surrender or do we continue till dusk?"

Greschwen spread bloodied fingers wide and pushed against the earth. Breathing heavily he raised his battered body to rest upright upon his knees; his grey bedraggled hair sitting wild about his shoulders.

"My Lord Volger," he gasped, "what in God's name do you want of me? Will you not call a halt to this slaughter, this unimaginable violation of life?"

A discerning eye would have caught the slight twitch of Volger's head as he began in a slow, quiet voice, so quiet that Greschwen struggled to hear. "I thought I made it quite clear what I want." A second, more pronounced tremor, accompanied a rapid transformation as his rising fury almost choked him. "*Your Kingdom*," he screamed, spittle bubbling at the corners of his thin-lipped mouth, as he glared with cold, grey eyes into Greschwen's upturned face. "I do not intend to remain here any longer suffering these intolerable conditions. The stench of you Eastlanders is worse than those of the Westland – but," he sneered, breathing deeply behind the scarlet cloth, "at least they offered some resistance. I had not expected to take your entire land within a matter of *weeks*." Volger's head twitched once more as his party supplied the expected mocking laughter.

"So Greschwen," he continued, straining now to compose himself and master the inner rage, the heat and the dampness of his skin, "after all, we might as well dispense with the 'King' bit – indeed, I will have to give much thought to your new position under my rule of the Eastland."

Greschwen tried desperately to stand, but his legs would not hold and he stumbled ungraciously back upon his knees. "Have mercy, my Lord, this slaughter is unnecessary, we are not warlike, we are a peaceable people, we have..."

Volger thrust his jaw forward. Members of his party exchanged anxious glances; their horses becoming restless as his rage refuelled. "A peaceable people!" He spat out the words. "You have no business being a peaceable people. You have failed in your duty as King. You make no preparations for war against an enemy as formidable as me. *It is an insult.*"

Volger clenched his teeth with such force that he grimaced at the pain which fired up through his jaw and into his temples. His nostrils flared as he dragged air frantically up into his head, as if to cool his burning brain: the heaving chest and scarlet flush upon his neck betraying the cost of the effort.

Though his impatience was still evident, he spoke in a softer, almost soothing tone. "Of course, this is of no consequence to you now," his breathing had become easier and the heat within his head was abating, "therefore," he continued, "I suggest you prepare to meet your maker, or whatever it is you do, and then we can depart this place – for there is *no* position for you under my rule of the Eastland."

Greschwen stared with raw, hollow eyes. "Dear God, you are truly as they said you were. You are without mercy and without sound mind. God deliver us, you are mad..."

"Take off his head," screamed Volger.

2

Kinfallon Castle rested on a craggy hillside, nestling in a purple carpet of late autumn heather, as the early morning mist snaked its way up from the river below.

A richly furnished bedroom high within the castle was dimly lit by the embers of a dying fire. Lord Aran, a dark curly-haired young man, lay sprawled upon a large, ornate, wooden-framed bed. A restless night of tossing and turning had left him tangled amongst the bedclothes, when he suddenly woke to the sound of approaching footsteps. Kicking his legs free of the clinging covers he grabbed a pillow, leapt from the bed, and positioned himself in readiness behind the door. Every second rendered him ever more awake as the stone floor chilled his feet.

The door opened slowly and a muscular blonde-haired youth crept into the room and approached the bed. Aran sprang from behind the door and began to batter his intruder with the pillow. Accompanied by much laughter the two tumbled head-first onto the bed and with thrashing arms and legs continued to wrestle.

Within minutes a laughing Matty shouted, "I surrender!"

"Totally and absolutely?" asked a grinning Aran, his chest heaving with the exertion.

"Totally and absolutely – never!" yelled Matty wriggling to be free, but finding himself held firm as Aran bound his upper body in the sheets.

Breathless, but happy with his conquest, Aran leapt from the bed and staggering across the room came to stand by the window. He marvelled at the changing images within the ethereal mist, as it continued to rise and thin before his eyes. Now he could just make out the hazy outline of the great pine trees that lined the edge of Felden Forest; unaware that eyes the colour of bronze were fixed upon him.

Having finally disentangled himself from his bindings, Matty lay at full stretch upon the bed.

"Only one week, Aran, to the final race of the season – all are to gather on the south side of the river and we have doubled the length of the course. The knights are game for the challenge and we have opened it up to all-comers – and Morven," Aran watched with amusement as Matty's face became heated, "has agreed to start the race and declare the winner – which has brought even more male blood to try their hand."

He rose quickly from the bed, stretched out his aching limbs, and joined his friend by the window.

Aran grinned. "I will win, you know."

"You may indeed win, my friend and master, but you will not be allowed to win, just because you are the son and heir, my Lord." Matty performed an exaggerated, grovelingly low bow, grabbed Aran behind both knees and threw him back onto the stone floor. Unable to contain his joy, Matty scrambled to his feet and made his escape through the open door.

Aran lay winded. He grinned. "I will win," he called after him. "So prepare to be a gallant loser or my sister may spurn your advances."

Enjoying the sensation of the cold stone cooling his skin, Aran remained upon the floor until his breathing eased. Eventually he rose and stood once more by the window. The mist had lifted, leaving nothing but a fine trail of gossamer lingering over the treetops, when an unexpected movement caught his eye.

It was the girl; the girl with hair the colour of amber, who stepped from the forest and looked up towards his window. Aran stared; his pulse lifting. She held his gaze with a gentle smile until a giant red stag, resplendent with fully mature white-tipped antlers, appeared behind her. Reaching out with a steady hand she pushed her fingers deep into the dense grey and white speckled fur that swaddled its throat. He watched in wonder as she turned her face towards the beast, looped her arm around its mighty neck and swung herself effortlessly up and onto its back. Aran felt his breath catch in his throat as she threw him a final glance, tossed her head towards the forest, and steered the mighty beast out of sight.

3

In the last room at the very top of Kinfallon Castle, the sorcerer Torpen was slumped in his ancient oak-carved armchair, amidst the most unimaginable chaos. His richly embroidered bright blue robes lay in folds over the tall, but now slight frame of an ageing body. His head nodded gently as if he were dozing, but his hands, long, bony and wrinkled with age bore witness to the tension coursing his veins as they gripped the smooth worn arms of his chair. At his feet lay his dog Ferneth: obedient, faithful old Ferneth, a beast as black as night but for white-tipped whiskers.

"Why should we of the Northland be so cursed?" muttered Torpen. "Why has there not been a son of the Tribe of Skea born to our land, to aid our people?" He shook his head and Ferneth flinched as the old man's agitation grew.

"I must have been blind. Indeed, we have all been blind. For how could we have missed the son, born to bring us hope, to stand with us in adversity?" He sighed then, so troubled a sigh that Ferneth raised her head and rested it gently upon his knees. The tension within the old man's body eased as he laid an ancient hand upon her soft ebony coat.

"Ah, of course, we need food. Too much fretting and not enough eating; we will fade away." Torpen gave a half-hearted smile, raised himself from his seat and threaded his way across the chaotic circular room. His chamber was cluttered with books of spells, of histories, mathematics and fables from afar. Tables were laden with potions and lotions and minerals both precious and otherwise. He stopped for a moment, having forgotten why he had risen from his seat, and then walked aimlessly on towards the window, drawing himself up to his full height as he leant upon the sill. His body stiffened: there was something in the woods to the south. Even with tired eyes he could clearly see something moving amongst the trees.

Ferneth pushed her cold wet nose up against the old man's gnarled hand and he shuffled backwards from the window, a mere flicker of a smile playing upon his lips as he began to retrace his steps.

"When the last race of the season is finally over, I must insist on speaking to the King. This inertia is a disease. As Volger moves ever further north, our plight grows deadlier. It is only a matter of time before he turns his attention to us."

Letting himself drop back once more into his chair, he pulled a green leather tome onto his knees; its fragile spine was fractured in many places and yet the faint gold inscription could still be seen: *The Legend of the Tribe of Skea*.

He opened the book and smoothed its aged pages with twisted fingers. "I do fear some disablement of our King that he should remain unmoved to prepare us for war." He straightened his crooked back as best he could.

"To oppose the King is treasonable, but, I ask myself, is it not worse to be remembered forever as Torpen, the Sorcerer of the Northland who failed his people? Who failed to find the one destined to be our saviour – to lead us into battle, to fight with us for our very existence?"

Ferneth sat before Torpen and placed both paws with some force onto the open book. Catching her eye, the old man chuckled, patted her affectionately and rose again, remembering at last that breakfast was long overdue.

4

For three days Balac had watched the sky above his house tell a sorry tale of death and destruction. The smoke, first black and dense, then grey and wispy, carried a multitude of ashen particles up to the heavens. They hung in the air gathering and jostling as if at play, until soft gusts of cooler air began to toss them about, transporting them every which way across the soft rolling hills of the Eastland, before drifting downwards to litter the land for miles around.

Having some years ago turned his back on the company of men, Balac had no desire to acquaint himself with the story behind this unnatural sky and the ash which fell to the earth around him.

He swung the axe with ease for the umpteenth time, but now his shoulders were beginning to ache. He was thankful that only half a dozen logs were left to be split and then he would have a stack big enough to get him through the winter. The light was just beginning to fade and his stomach tightened in anticipation, as the faint aroma of the hare stew simmering on the stove drifted through the air.

As he positioned the last log before him, he caught sight of the first wolf in his peripheral vision. It was a he-wolf, large and dark, standing at the edge of the woodland peering out across the clearing which surrounded Balac's home. Balac sensed more movement amongst the trees and knew in his heart that this was a pack of some size. He rolled his shoulders backwards, easing out the tired muscles, and drew air in deeply through his nostrils.

He smiled inwardly and muttered under his breath, "May as well get the job done." And with that Balac lifted the axe high, swung it through the air and brought the blade crashing down, straight through the centre of the log. The two halves flew upwards into the air and fell some way off. Hoping this would act as a distraction, he turned ready to run, only to find himself confronted by a she-wolf who stood teeth bared and spinal hair on high, blocking his route to safety.

She was a magnificent beast with a golden chest and dark snout which she lifted provocatively, as if inviting him to appreciate her beauty before she pounced. As his startling green eyes met her own, she launched herself into the air and with one leap pinned him to the ground.

"You are such a hussy," Balac yelled, as she covered his face with long lingering licks from her rough hot tongue. "And what in hell's name have you been eating to give you such foul breath?"

Balac twisted his face this way and that, struggling to free himself from her grip. "Hey, Kyler," he called, "get over here and give a man a hand. Your woman has no modesty."

Balac began to laugh out loud and Akir stopped her passionate licking, stretched her jaws wide and belched full in his face. By the time Balac had finally managed to free himself from Akir's embrace, Kyler had led the pack out into the clearing. Balac wandered amongst them, laying a hand upon each, speaking nonsense in low soothing tones.

As darkness fell, Kyler and Akir lay beside Balac as he sat on the steps leading to his door, greedily devouring the contents of the steaming pot. He assumed the pack had had good hunting, as not one of the beasts approached him in anticipation of a morsel of food. However, he could not help but be a little perturbed by the passing thought that perhaps his cooking was so bad that they would rather go hungry.

Balac frowned, and reaching forward, picked a speck of ash from Akir's soft golden throat and rubbed it between his finger and thumb. The dark grease spread and stained his skin.

5

Outside Kinfallon Castle, Aran and Matty mingled with the crowds. There was much energy in the air as the young men jostled, laughed and goaded one another with boasts and counter-boasts. The day was dry and bright but gathering storm clouds in the north looked threatening. The wind was lifting and a chill in the air foretold of a winter fast approaching.

Standing in the midst of the throng, Aran found himself peering towards the forest over the heads of those around him. He felt certain that she would run again this year, staying within the shadows of the mighty pines, and yet outpacing the official runners with ease. Aran moved out towards the edge of the crowd, his stomach tightening. Was she there, perhaps smiling, perhaps laughing at them? He felt his throat thicken and in his nervousness he laughed out loud.

"Why so hysterical, brother?" Morven tapped him on the shoulder. "Hysterics is supposed to be the preserve of the female, you know." She smiled up into his handsome face, noticing his high colour and the brightness of his eyes. "Good luck Aran, I think this year you will need it for Matty is determined that he will clip your heels and take you on the uphill finish."

"Take care, sister, where you place your wager. I have a trick or two of my own."

Morven followed his gaze. "Is she there?" She peered past him and glared out into the forest. "She makes fools of you all; she must be possessed to run as she does."

"Don't," he said, his face suddenly darkening. "You know how easily rumour spreads."

Morven flushed, and turning quickly from him, addressed the crowd. "To the bravest and the best of Kinfallon, I declare the final race before the fall of the winter solstice to be upon us."

As she sounded the gong, a mighty roar rose from the expectant crowd. With her female entourage close behind, Morven headed back towards the castle. They ran through the great hallway and, lifting their brightly coloured skirts, ascended the vast winding stone staircase laughing as they went. Once at the vantage point, red-faced and panting for breath, Morven shrieked with joy as she saw Matty appear over the brow of the hill ahead of the pack. "Yes, Matty, you can do it!" Her dark hair danced with delight as she jumped up and down, willing him on.

Aran, meantime, had given the race little thought, being preoccupied from the outset in trying to catch a glimpse of the girl. They had gone less than fifty yards when he caught sight of her, marvelling at the ease and pace of her movement. Taking a deep breath he lifted his speed, abandoned the race, and headed straight for the trees. His eyes took a moment to adjust as he left the brightness of the day and plunged into the shadows. She was there, just a few paces ahead of him, and his heart lifted. She glanced back over her shoulder, her amber hair swaying with the movement, and then effortlessly increased her speed and headed deeper into the forest. Aran followed, but quickly began to realise that she was moving ever further away from him, when suddenly she simply vanished before his eyes.

Gasping for air, he stopped abruptly and dropped to his knees. His body heaved in rhythm with his breath as he drew air rapidly in and out through his mouth and nostrils. As he waited for his breathing to reach a gentler pace, he fell back onto his heels and surveyed the scene around him. A rustle of leaves caused him to turn and there, some distance away to his left, he beheld a stag. He wondered, as he watched the mighty beast, whether this could be the same stag that had taken the girl on his back. Aran found himself transfixed by the vision and the realisation that the stag was staring straight at him.

Becoming aware of the sound of running water close by, he drew his gaze away from the beast and rose to his feet. Glancing back over his shoulder, he was not surprised to find that the creature was nowhere to be seen.

By the brook he knelt to raise cupped hands of cool water to his lips. And then he saw her, sat on the opposite side of the stream, her amber hair and tunic of brown leather moulding her to the autumn landscape.

"You run well, Lord Aran," she said in a light clear voice.

He held her gaze.

"That may be so," he replied, "but not so well as you. You appear to have a gift."

"Or a curse – depending on your point of view."

"Who are you?" Aran asked, as he rose to his feet.

She laughed and reddened a little. "My name is Jesyka."

He smiled, only too aware of the colour in his own cheeks, and the fire within his stomach.

"Your sister would say I am the crazy girl who lives in the forest, runs like the wind, and no doubt dances with the Devil."

"You are probably right," he shrugged. "But she is no different to many who fear what they do not understand."

He watched as she backed away from the stream and felt for a moment that she had disappeared again. But no, she was still there. Merely a trick of the light, he thought. "I remember when I first saw you," he continued, "over a year ago now in the market-place. I remember you were with an older woman. Your mother, perhaps?"

"Perhaps," she teased.

"You wore a hood, it slipped and your hair…" he paused, "this I also remember."

Aran watched as Jesyka stooped to retrieve the cloak she had been sitting on, throw it around her shoulders, and step effortlessly over the stream to stand beside him.

"Now that you have lost the race you have no need to run, so perhaps we could walk?"

They moved away from the water and walked some twenty paces together before either spoke again.

"The woman you saw me with was my mother, Methna. My family has lived here in your glorious forest for many years. We have walked your streets, bartered in your marketplace and gossiped with your people. We know all there is to know about King Broehain and his family. And," she smiled, "when I come to Kinfallon, I am only seen if I wish to be seen."

"How is that so?" asked Aran.

And then without warning she was gone.

Aran spun around. His head swinging left to right, up and down; eyes wide and mouth gaping. Initially stunned into silence, he regained his wits quickly and called out. "Jesyka," he yelled. "Jesyka."

Before he saw her, he heard her laughter, as she stepped away from the trunk of a mighty pine and appeared before him.

"Dear Lord, are you human? Are you bewitched?" he exclaimed.

Fearing she would disappear again he stared long and hard into eyes of pure amber, in an attempt to bind her to the spot.

"Yes to your first question, and no to your second," she finally responded; attempting to check the amusement in her voice as she beheld his confusion. "I seemingly have a second gift or curse – I can merge with my surroundings and take on the stillness and hue of any object. It was fun as a child to outrun my parents and then disappear. However, I was severely scolded for not using my 'gifts' appropriately – one lesson among many that I have had to learn."

"Are you then…" he paused, watching her golden eyes blaze with excitement, "who I think you are?"

"As I do not possess the gift of mindreading, perhaps you will say more?"

He hesitated. "Can the 'son' of the Tribe of Skea be a girl – a woman?"

"No," she offered flatly. "But a woman can be the heir of Skea – for men's minds have become narrow. The legend does not speak of the son of the Tribe of Skea, it speaks of the heir – but as all are expecting a male, and those that have gone before have all, to my knowledge, been male, the assumption has rewritten the legend."

Aran struggled momentarily to accept that the suspicion he had held for so long could indeed be true. "Then you are the one Torpen has been searching for? My people have been waiting for your coming for so long that I can hardly believe you have been here so close and not made yourself known."

Jesyka sighed. "Whilst you are perceptive, Lord Aran, and so have discovered the heir for yourself, you are also obviously not well versed in the terms of the Deed of Covenant that my ancestors made on Mount Valhallion. I cannot reveal myself, I can only be found by those who truly seek with an open heart and mind, and whose need is great. Whilst I strive to serve those who invite me to come amongst them, at my coming is an added danger – for if I am eliminated this would render the Northlanders even more vulnerable. The knowledge of my demise would take from your people what Volger fears most. A people who believe they can defeat him. A people full of hope."

Aran watched her closely. "Is the danger of Volger so dreadful? Is he truly as evil a warlord as the stories tell?"

Jesyka's face lost not only its smile but some of its radiance. "I do not need to know what stories have reached this far north to know that they can in no way do justice to the depravity of this man."

"Then there can be no time to lose. Will you come with me now to Kinfallon Castle and speak with my father? Torpen has called yet another meeting to appeal to him to act with all haste in this matter and with the knowledge that the heir is among us, surely…"

"No, Aran," she spoke gently, stepping towards him and placing her hand upon his shoulder. "I will not leave the safety of the forest until I know that your father believes in me and desires my presence at his Court. I beg of you for my safety and yours that you will attend the meeting and present your suspicion that I could be the one Torpen has been seeking. If there is an agreement to put this suspicion to the test, come to Felden Forest under cover of darkness tonight and bring only Torpen, Matty, your sister and your father – and we will see before the dawn breaks if there is hope for any of us."

"But how will we find you?"

"There will be no need – *we* will find you."

Aran raised his hand and instinctively laid it over her own as it rested still upon his shoulder. Voices could be heard in the distance calling his name.

"Until tomorrow, Lord Aran," she whispered, before she withdrew her hand and was gone.

6

Torpen, with Ferneth at his heels and the green tome cradled in his arms, entered the Great Hall to find some twelve men and Lady Morven gathered before a roaring fire which hissed and spat as new timbers were laid.

"And so, Torpen, we are summoned to yet another gathering. And to do what, pray? Listen to you berate us, again, upon our collective failure?" King Broehain spoke with arms outstretched as if in jest, but the irritation in his voice was evident.

"You may speak less lightly my Lord when Volger is at our gates and we have no resistance to offer," the old man replied, as he shuffled towards the long trestle table at the centre of the room. Determined to warm his old bones as best he could, Torpen occupied the seat nearest to the fire. Sensing an ill-tempered meeting, the others exchanged furtive looks as they took their places at the table.

"I fear, gentleman, and Lady Morven," Torpen nodded graciously towards her as she sat on the left of her father, "that we have not engaged with the level of energy and passion that we should have in our quest to discover the whereabouts of our heir of the Tribe of Skea." There were audible intakes of breath and uneasy glances in the King's direction.

"I predict," Torpen continued, "that we have only one winter before Volger turns his attention to the Northland."

"We do not know that he will come," Morven offered, but would not meet Torpen's gaze. "Perhaps he will be content with his gains in the south."

Torpen struggled to control his frustration. "Lady Morven, it is not a matter of *if*, but only of *when*."

King Broehain breathed deeply, rose slowly to his feet and with a weary voice addressed them all. "If we prepare for war, our losses will be mighty. If he is, as all say, a most vicious enemy then would it not be, as King, my duty to attempt a peaceful way forward? If we had been blessed with a son of the Tribe of Skea then perhaps our choices could have been different but this has not been our fate. And why is that?" He looked from one to the other.

"Perhaps, father, because we have not been looking in the right place."

Broehain glared as his son. "Aran, we will not discuss that woman again. I forbid you from wasting the Court's time with your obsession with the girl in the forest."

Aran absorbed his father's displeasure and pressed on. "Torpen, what does it say about the descendent of the Tribe of Skea? Read it again so that the Court can decide whether the girl in the forest could be the heir."

Broehain's fist hit the table. "Dear God! Will I be defied in my own Court, by my own son, in the presence of my own Council? I forbid that we speak of this matter."

Torpen's eyes brightened, he sat forward in his chair and spoke soothingly, "My Lord, my King, would it not be better for the Council to debate the boy's theory? For then we could dismiss his claim, as I am sure we will."

Morven placed a calming hand upon her father's arm and bent her head to speak softly in his ear. "Perhaps, Father, if the girl's whereabouts were revealed, she would then be finally exposed as a witch, or a harlot, or indeed both, and my brother may at last be shamed into coming to his senses."

Torpen opened the book before him and cleared his throat. "The legend of the Tribe of Skea is known to you all; we have grown up with this legend as part of our folklore. It has been passed by the spoken word, even beyond these shores. I have met many a traveller who has spoken of the legend, somewhat embellished at times, as is the wont of stories told and retold."

Torpen became aware that Ferneth had slipped from under the table and that something held her attention as she paced up and down before the closed door.

"But here," he placed his hands palms down upon his beloved book, "here we have one of four identical tomes passed down to the four nephews of Tamlin as documentation of the true legend – undefiled."

Torpen raised his shoulders. "I, Torpen, am the keeper of the legend for the Northland, my brother Borden for the Westland, Calfed for the Eastland and poor unfortunate Wensele, was the keeper for the Southland." He paused for effect, conscious that he now had everyone's attention.

"It is told in these pages that an ancient tribe of this land, the Tribe of Skea, was a people admired and honoured across the centuries as a people of peace and justice. However, it was also common knowledge," he raised his voice and directed his words in the King's direction, "that when all else failed, they would defend to the death their way of life and were esteemed throughout the Great Crossland as noble warriors who knew no equal. The legend tells that after a turbulent period spanning many decades of war, the elders of the Tribe of Skea climbed Mount Valhallion, in the desolate northern wastes of the Northland and prayed to God in their anguish and suffering for the means to bring peace to their land. The legend tells that when they returned they told of how they had been blessed and that they had been gifted a living prophecy."

Ferneth was still pacing and becoming more agitated, as Torpen began to read: *"The descendants of the Tribe of Skea will scatter throughout the four nations of the Great Crossland and in each generation an heir born of the blood of the Skea Tribe will be blessed with special gifts. Each of the four nations will have their own heir who will be a blessing to their adopted people and will offer them in times of great need and persecution, the fortitude, skill, wisdom and courage to face their foes. It will be the destiny of those born to fulfil this role that they will be possessed of a heart, mind and spirit that will be fed by those who have gone before them."*

The old man was breathing more heavily now. *"Whether at war or at peace the gifted ones will be ever waiting and ready to serve when a nation reaches out to them in truth and belief. Only when those in true need are themselves open in heart, mind and spirit will they be able to see clearly the true heir destined to be at one with them."* He paused. *"But, if the eye of the beholder looks but will not see, the heir will not be revealed to them and they will continue in their blindness to the end."*

Torpen slumped back into his chair and slammed the book shut.

Animated discussion broke out around the table, until Broehain's raised voice silenced them all. "And so, Torpen, I listen and yet I hear nothing new."

Aran, his face aglow, pushed back his chair and rose to his feet. "The legend speaks of an heir, not a son. There is nothing in the legend that excludes the possibility of the heir being a woman."

Morven sneered. "And you seriously believe that the girl in the forest is the one, a true descendant from the Tribe of Skea?"

Aran hesitated. "I do, for I have spoken with her this day and am without doubt that she is possessed of gifts beyond our understanding. She speaks with a maturity, an assuredness beyond her years. And I believe she is the one Torpen has been seeking."

Raised voices outwith the chamber drowned those within, as three heavy blows rained upon the door. Ferneth backed away as the metal latch clicked open and a tall stooped stranger entered the room.

All at the table rose at the intrusion and turned to face him.

"What in God's name is it that cannot wait when the Council is in session?" called Broehain.

The man's face was ashen and his eyes haunted; his boots were laden with mud and his cloak, torn and slipping from his shoulders, was steadied by a trembling hand.

"My Lords, King Broehain," he rasped. "I bring desperate news from the lowlands. Your border people are fleeing their homes and moving further north. Whole villages are on the move. They carry what they can but have abandoned much of what they own."

There was a tremor upon his lips as he finally focussed upon the sea of faces before him. "For the Eastland has fallen and fires rage across the length and breadth of its land."

Exhaustion finally overcame him and the man slipped to his knees. Moving swiftly, Aran and Matty raised the man up and guided him to a seat by the fire.

"They speak," he continued, "of survivors crossing the border with harrowing tales of one called Volger. They say he calls himself the Supreme Ruler, not only of the Eastland but also of the South and West. They say that all have fallen…"

"And what of King Gerschwen?" asked Broehain in a low voice.

"They say he was most cruelly dealt with, my Lord. His head hacked from his shoulders as he pleaded for mercy for his people."

7

Sitting high in a clear autumn sky, a narrow crescent moon offered little comfort to the riders who moved cautiously through the blackened woodland. The crunch of hooves upon frostbitten leaves chartered their progress as the night grew ever darker.

"Brother," Matty whispered, reaching with a gloved hand to grasp Aran's arm, "we have embarked on many a foolhardy jaunt together, but this has to be sheer madness. We have been going round in circles this past hour." Aran felt Matty increase the pressure of his grip. "Listen to me Aran, she is not here. She is not coming."

Aran felt a rush of air at his back, as the rhythmic sound of beating wings approached at speed from behind. A large eagle with a six-foot wingspan swooped low over the riders, spooking the horses and chilling the air. As they watched the eagle's progress, it landed but a short way ahead on the roof of a low thatched cottage with smoke rising from its chimney.

Torpen blinked and stared ahead with wide eyes. "What magic is this? That cottage, it was not there but a moment ago – unless my old eyes are deceiving me?" He blinked again.

"They are no more deceived than my young eyes, Torpen. There was no cottage," said Matty warily, as he stared ahead.

"That, if I am not mistaken is a silver-backed eagle."
Aran could not hide his excitement. "I cannot think that
one has ever been seen this far north – it is the symbol of
the people of the Southland. How magnificent!"

Light began to spill from the cottage, as the door opened
and the sound of voices, unusual sounding voices, escaped
into the night. The riders dismounted and, leading their
horses forward, found themselves drawn towards the golden
glow and the suggestion of warmth inside.

A woman's voice called out. "You are most welcome,
honoured guests, please enter my home and rest a while."

They hesitated.

"Who speaks?" whispered Morven to Aran. "I see no-one,
is it her, is that her voice?"

"My name is Methna, Lady Morven – I am the mother
of the one you seek."

Aran cleared his throat. "I have brought my father, King
Broehain, to meet with Jesyka. Is she with you? Can we
speak with her?"

Methna stepped into the doorway; a shock of golden
curls hung about her shoulders, as a fitted jacket of finest
hide, the colour of ripe chestnuts, sat above a heavy scarlet
skirt.

"She is here, but you must cross our threshold, for only
then can we guarantee your safety and ours." Methna peered
with inquisitive pale brown eyes into the darkness beyond
them, and then stepped aside to bid them enter.

Torpen was the first to move forward. "This is all very
promising, very promising indeed."

"God help us," said Matty as he followed the old man
into the light. "All very odd, more like."

******

What appeared from the outside to be a small two-roomed cottage was on the inside a space some four times larger than any one of them had imagined. Their senses were assailed by strange sights, smells and indeed strange-looking people. They found themselves in a room lit by an open fire and four large ornate metal candelabra: each suspended from the ceiling by a hefty chain and throwing soft light into every corner of the room.

Methna led her visitors towards a low copper-topped table which glimmered in the light and offered its intricate carvings of animals, plants, mountains and trees for admiration. Ceramic dishes of varying sizes in highly glazed bright colours adorned the table, offering a variety of spiced fragrant cakes as warm wine was poured into heavily jewelled goblets by a small man with sallow skin and cat-like eyes. He bowed deeply, stepped back from the table, and with easy agility settled himself cross-legged into one of the many low, deeply padded seats which surrounded the circle of copper.

Methna smiled. "You must excuse the strangeness of the company I keep. We are what you might call 'a mixed bag,'" she said, as two more men stepped forward and joined the gathering.

The larger of the two also bore a sallow complexion, framed within raven black hair that lay in an intricately woven plait over his left shoulder. The plait was fixed with straps of leather adorned with coloured beads and a train of eagle feathers that reached below his waist. His stature spoke of strength, with the extensive bulk of his torso hidden beneath a blanket of red and black and held at the shoulder by a clasp fashioned from leather and bone. Aran watched with wide eyes, as a hand decorated with fine intricate lines of black dye reached out from beneath the blanket and lifted a goblet from the table before him.

Morven steered King Broehain forward. "Come, father, sit here close by the fire. Take some wine. I fear the night air has chilled you to the bone."

"Please do all partake of something to eat and drink," offered Methna. "We sadly could not have revealed our location any sooner, not, that is, until Sirus," she pointed towards the roof, "our friend from the Southland, was satisfied that we were safe to do so. Unfortunately Volger's spies are more able and cunning than we would wish, but Sirus will keep watch over us this night and if danger approaches he will raise the alarm."

Torpen appeared invigorated, his eyes alive and his cheeks suddenly aglow. "This is splendid. At last real help is at hand. Come, come we have much to discuss."

Aran's voice betrayed his impatience. "It was Jesyka that we came to see. I met your daughter in the forest yesterday. She asked that I bring my father. You said she was here."

"Yes, Lord Aran, all this I know and I commend you on fulfilling your task." She smiled broadly, but then fixed him with a determined look. "However, I speak honestly when I say I do not know if I am more pleased or saddened that you have finally come for my daughter's help."

She paused. "Do not be offended by my plain speaking – we have little time and as Torpen states, much to discuss. For although we have only just met, we have merely hours in which to decide whether we will stand together," her face darkened, "most likely unto death – or whether *we* will take our leave of your land at the break of dawn and *you* will be left to forge your own history unaided."

Aran followed Matty's gaze towards the bags and weaponry stacked by the door, no doubt in readiness for a hasty departure.

"This is true, very true," interrupted Torpen, "but if we could speak with Jesyka."

"Jesyka will come," Methna stated firmly.

After a moment she raised her goblet to all present and offered a toast. "To the Northland, may we defend her with honour in her hour of need, if this is indeed to be our destiny." One by one they raised their goblets, exchanged glances, and drank to the toast. Broehain was the last to lift the warm wine to his lips, and the last to replace his cup, still half full, to the table before him.

The third man who made up Methna's 'mixed bag' was tall and dark and wore the clothes of a prince from the desert lands. Aran marvelled at the finery of his silken delicately embroidered robes which peeped out from beneath a full-length sumptuous grey fur coat. His black leather boots were set with precious stones, their beauty only partially revealed through small incisions in the outer skin.

"And now, my friends, to business," said Zabian, his voice rich and deep in tone; as his dark lively eyes flitted from one to another as he spoke. "We have been made aware that messengers were repeatedly sent over many months from the Southland into the East, the West and the Northland requesting assistance. This we are told has been ongoing ever since Volger's war parties first landed upon the southern shores many months ago."

"I know nothing of such matters," said Aran, the colour rising in his cheeks. "These messengers of which you speak, they did not reach our Court – no request to my knowledge was ever made to the Northland. Father, this is as I say, is it not?"

Broehain was slow to respond. "I have never received such a request. It is as my son states."

"And if you had?" enquired Methna.

Broehain remained silent.

"So, you received no requests for help," Zabian paused, a slight frown forming across his brows, "but the West did and did nothing, and the East did and did nothing," he sighed, "and this, my friends, is what Volger thrives on, this 'nothingness'. Man's inability to act on behalf of his fellow man."

He smiled. "So now you have a little problem – because now you have no one to call to your aid but us. And we are here solely because of Jesyka, for while she lives hope lives – and if hope lives, my friends, you may, just may, have a chance."

Broehain moved forward in his seat and stared before him at no one in particular. "Is she truly as the legend tells a descendent of the Tribe of Skea? Are you all without doubt on this matter?"

Zabian smiled and caught Methna's eye. "Having imparted to her many of the skills that we possess," he explained, "we know first-hand of her strength and courage. Her true lineage can be traced back to the Tribe of Skea through her father, Raghnall – and her commitment to your cause is evidenced by her years of painstaking preparation for the task she has always known she may one day be asked to fulfil."

"I heard word, years ago now…" Broehain hesitated, "that the heir was dead."

There was a hiss from the fire, as if someone had spat into its glowing embers.

Methna rose suddenly and gestured the need for silence. Zabian slid his hands into the tops of his boots and, grasping the golden hilts of two razor-sharp daggers, began to draw them out. Choi, still cross-legged and with an ivory long-stemmed pipe clamped between his teeth, gracefully lifted his arms in slow motion and, reaching backwards over his shoulders, raised two blades merely inches from the scabbards strapped to his back. Aran held his breath, as he listened to the quickening rhythm of his heart thumping against the stillness. Daring to lift his eyes, he stole a glance in his father's direction and witnessed a single bead of sweat spring to life upon his temple.

There came scratching on the roof and all eyes went heavenwards. Methna's body relaxed as she gently blew a soft stream of air out through pursed lips and reformed a smile. "Either a near miss or a false alarm – either way, we must push on."

Having listened intently to their discussion, Jesyka decided to step away from the cottage wall and reveal her whereabouts. Aran was the first to see her and rose to his feet.

"Sometimes," said Zabian, "it would be good to know where you are before you leap out and give one of your devoted guardians a severe fright."

"Firstly, I did not leap and secondly it is always good to have your reflexes tested once in a while – especially as one gets older." Jesyka grinned in his direction, as moving further into the room, she stopped beside her mother and rested a hand upon her shoulder.

"King Broehain, allow me to present my daughter, Jesyka," said Methna.

He raised tired, anxious eyes to meet her.

"This meeting has been a long time in coming, my Lord," she offered. "I, and my somewhat unusual, but believe me priceless, comrades-in-arms, are at your service if this is your will?" Jesyka inclined her head.

"I had hoped for peace – perhaps to negotiate," he blurted out.

"This I understand, others have tried this before you, but it is not possible," Jesyka replied. "You must believe all that you have heard of Volger's infamy."

"That my father desires to spare his people much suffering is an honourable course of action," declared Morven.

"But is unobtainable and therefore clearly foolish," stated Jesyka firmly, holding Morven's hostile glare. "There is little honour in leaving a people defenceless and in ignorance in some false belief that somehow all will be well."

"I believe King Greschwen attempted such a strategy – did he not?" added Methna.

"Father, I believe in Jesyka and her guardians; for they come before us offering their lives in service to our people." Aran spoke with passion, but his father refused to meet his stare. "Their knowledge is far greater than ours, their worldliness beyond our knowing. But even if this venture is unto death for us all, surely it is better for the Northlanders to fight than be slaughtered like pigs." Aran's dark eyes darted round the assembled company. "Come Torpen, what say you?"

"I am saddened that we were blind to your presence for so long, Jesyka," offered Torpen, "and although it may be almost too late, we, gathered here this night, are all that stands in the way of Volger inflicting a darker age than has ever been known." He sighed. "Perhaps from which we may never recover."

Morven battled tears. "My father's decision must be the final word – do you forget that *he* is the King!"

For a few heartbeats no one spoke.

"The choice, King Broehain, is indeed yours, as your daughter rightly states," said Methna.

Morven turned to Aran. "Besides, what actual proof do we have that *all* is as they say?"

"And if you had proof, what then?" asked Jesyka.

All eyes turned to King Broehain and remained upon him, until he finally spoke. "Then, I would, in my people's name and for my people's sake, ask for your service in our cause."

Aran felt his skin glow, as Jesyka threw him a triumphant smile. He watched as she placed her open palms on the copper-topped table, and leaning forward peered into his father's listless eyes. What was she searching for? Perhaps for some affirmation of life within, or merely confirmation that he meant what he said? She stifled a sigh and turned to meet Morven's cold, defiant expression.

"Then we will get your proof," said Jesyka, stepping back from the table. "Our party must be small and able. Three days hence at dawn I will travel south with," she nodded to each in turn, "Nunca, Choi, Zabian, Aran, Matty," she hesitated, "and Morven."

Broehain was suddenly animated. "Not Morven, this I cannot contemplate. My wife, I have already lost my wife."

"I must insist, my Lord, for it is obvious that it is Morven's testimony alone that you will value and therefore I give you my word that we will value her life above our own in order to bring that testimony safely home."

* * * * * *

It was almost dawn when the Northlanders finally rode out of the forest; each alone with their thoughts of what had occurred and what was to come.

Methna stood beside Jesyka in the doorway of the cottage, as Sirus called out into the morning air, circled overhead, and with his task complete set a steady course southward and home. Rion, with an orange glow from the rising sun climbing steadily behind him, stood on Kinfallon Hill looking out across Felden Forest. As Sirus rose higher into the lightening sky, Rion raised his mighty head and bellowed a fervent farewell.

"And I am to remain here – and wait?" queried Methna, as she placed an arm around her daughter's waist.

"Now that you can walk freely abroad, mother, you will be able to judge the mood of the people first-hand. Befriend

Broehain in Morven's absence, if you can, for all is not as it should be in the royal household."

Jesyka watched Sirus' progress until he was no more than a black spot upon the morning. "But above all..."

"Yes, I know, wait for your father." Methna smiled, but her eyes grew moist. "He has been away too long." She shook her head as if to dislodge an unwanted thought. "Your own quest, however, is not without its dangers – so take care, my daughter, for there is one, I fear, who will betray you."

8

The Abbey of Iola sat on a fine grassy headland that looked out across the forbidding Eastern Sea. The harbour and picturesque bay which sat beneath the imposing Abbey had been home for centuries to a thriving fishing and shipbuilding community. Overhead a sky of ashen coloured clouds, buffeted by a swirling squally wind, delivered occasional tunnels of light to the troubled earth below.

Volger set a pernicious pace as he marched through the lofty walkways of the Abbey; his son Kamron, pulled along by the force of his father's will, could not match the length of his stride and found himself awkwardly requiring to take two steps to match his father's one. Kamron's breathing became laboured and he wished to throw off the heavy mantel of his finest winter cloak but dared not falter in his step. Some commented that his physical likeness to his father was uncanny, and yet the soft hazel eyes challenged the severity of his pale skin and over-large jaw.

They turned now and began to make their way down the aisle towards the high altar; the entourage behind them paring down to no more than three abreast as the beat of their marching boots echoed through the vaulted ceiling above.

A woman in a dark grey habit knelt before the altar, her head slightly inclined, as gentle rhythmic murmuring escaped dry, anxious lips. Volger stopped; his cold eyes narrowing as they beheld the many gold and bejewelled artefacts that adorned the altar.

"So, Mother Abbess, I take it you have now had sufficient time to consider my request which I fully understand is no doubt not to your liking – but such is the curse of the defeated."

When she made no immediate reply, Volger found himself staring at the back of her head as his irritation grew and he began to pace the mosaic floor directly behind her.

"I grant that you are not acquainted with my ways, but be assured this is me at my most lenient. I have set my mind on using the Abbey as my base during my time in the Eastland. Your Order is therefore required to vacate forthwith."

He stopped pacing, his eyes remaining fixed on the grey figure as he waited for a response. His foot began to tap incessantly upon the tiles and his long fingers caressed the silver hilt of the sword strapped to his side. The murmuring ceased as the Abbess rose to her feet; she was slight in frame and height, but the strength of defiance in her eyes halted the tapping foot.

"This is a house of God, and has been for over five hundred years," her voice held steady. "What you ask is unthinkable please take your war outside the walls of my Abbey."

Volger rolled his head as if stretching out a stiff neck, and threw a dark look in Kamron's direction. "Obviously I have not made myself clear. This is not a negotiation; I am no longer asking you, I am now telling you…" His voice was climbing now in volume as the hateful heat started to creep over his body. "Because this is no longer your Abbey – it is *mine* – along with every golden bauble in it."

Screaming gulls circled high overhead, wailing out their mournful song as the Abbess stood before her tormentor in silent contempt. Volger turned abruptly away and moved towards the altar. Without taking his eyes from the golden candelabra encrusted with rubies and ablaze with light, he spoke again.

"More importantly," his breathing appeared a little heavier, but the voice was calmer, the tone subdued, "let us not forget the other matter that we discussed." Before her lips had even parted to respond, he raised his hand. "I will hear no more. I do not expect you to relish what you are required to do. I merely expect you to do it." He picked with a pointed fingernail at the small specks of cold hardened wax that stained the altar cloth.

"Besides," he turned back to face her, as those still defiant eyes held back the tears, "it will mean that you may stay on a little longer in your beloved Abbey." He shrugged, clamped his arm around Kamron's shoulders and turning the boy about, headed back along the aisle.

Throwing back his head, he delivered a warning. "Think on this, Mother Abbess: if you do not oblige me in this matter, the full complement of your Order may be required to take a short stroll off those magnificent Iola cliffs."

9

Balac had pondered his dilemma ever since the black smoke had first appeared in the sky. He knew, only too well, the likely horror of its origins, but also knew that it was doubtful he could survive the winter without venturing beyond his forest home to replenish his food stocks. So deep ran his desire to remain isolated and unburdened by the world of men that he continued to ruminate over his predicament, until he suddenly remembered the fish. Dear God, how could he have forgotten the fish?

On his last trip to Iola, some months earlier, he had taken a notion to visit the much talked of smokery which sat close by the Abbey steps. It was a warm sunny afternoon when Balac arrived to find Old Cal the proprietor packing away his stall, having sold all but two small fish. On realising that Balac had never tasted an oak smoked herring, Cal promptly broke open the moist golden fish between his hefty brown stained fingers and revealed the white delicate flesh beneath the smoky exterior. The heavenly smell drew Balac closer and he found himself unable to resist the proffered morsel.

He had eagerly purchased the remaining fish and placed an order with Old Cal for two dozen more. Having secured this transaction with a generous deposit, Balac had agreed to return and take possession of the fish before the winter solstice.

The memory of the smell, the taste and the anticipation of twenty four of the golden beauties enhancing his winter food stock could not now be erased. After all, he could surely enter Iola early one morning, complete his business, and depart without involving himself in the affairs of its people.

10

As the moon and stars grew ever brighter in a darkening midnight sky, three figures wearing dark hooded cloaks slipped by a dozing sentry and entered Kinfallon Castle.

"This is not good," whispered Zabian, as the three started to mount the staircase to the upper chambers. "This is child's play; their security is a joke."

They stopped: aware of approaching voices.

"You were saying?" whispered Jesyka, raising an eyebrow as she grabbed at both their cloaks and pulling them swiftly up against the cold grey granite rendered them lost to the seeing world. The two knights passed within a whisker of their location and the three pressed hastily on.

Jesyka hesitated just for a moment outside Aran's room, dropped the hood of her cloak onto her shoulders, shook her hair free, and stepped inside. The chamber was dimly lit but she could clearly see that the bed was unoccupied. As she moved further into the room she found him sat on the edge of a high-backed tapestry chair staring at the last throes of a dying fire. He was wrapped in a richly embroidered cover that he had taken from the bed, but his legs and feet were bare. Roused now from his troublesome thoughts by his midnight intruder, he knew at a glance that it was Jesyka's silhouette in the darkness and his heart leapt.

"Are you a bad sleeper?" she asked with a smile.

"Only since you filled my head with so much to think on," he replied.

She threw off the cloak and continued across the room until she stood before him blocking the light and the little warmth from the fire. He slid back onto the chair, aware of the heat growing through his body. She wore a breastplate of boiled hide with the burnt etching of the head of a stag centre stage; above her left shoulder he noted the feathered tops of a dozen arrows; a miniature bow unlike anything he had seen before hung from her hip and strapped to the outer side of both legs he noted a collection of horn handles depicting the whereabouts of: two, four, six, eight short-bladed daggers and the matt grey ornately crafted handle of a shortened broadsword stood proud at her right shoulder.

"By your attire, I take it we leave tonight?" queried Aran. "But you said three days hence, did you not?"

"I did," she responded with a nod. "But on reflection, we decided to amend our plans in the hope of remaining one step ahead of our enemy. If somehow our security was breached, and word reaches Volger that we intend to pay him a visit, we may still retain an element of surprise if we leave without delay."

"My sister will create merry hell – how do you imagine you will get her to comply?"

"We have given that task to Nunca." She smiled. "Perhaps we should take a moment and pray for him?"

Aran stifled a laugh and rose to his feet. He walked away from her and pulling the cover from his shoulders threw it onto the bed, grabbed his clothes from the floor where he had discarded them and began to dress.

Jesyka turned hastily away and sitting down hard in the vacant chair fixed her eyes upon the dying embers.

* * * * * *

45

Choi waited, small as he was, by crouching amongst the dense undergrowth which grew in ugly untamed clumps close by the river. With a keen ear he noted: one man, large in size, approaching from inland.

"Nunca, so light on your feet for one so big," he whispered with a frown, "but not light enough."

Nunca ignored his comments and headed straight for the boat, carrying Morven in his arms wrapped in his red and black blanket. He set her on her feet. She ignored them both, looked back over her shoulder towards the castle with a dark despondent stare, and clutching the blanket to her, stepped silently into the boat.

"What?" whispered Choi. "No fuss?"

Nunca shrugged as if bewildered by her complicity and arranged the canvas to cover her from view. Within seconds Zabian had also appeared, accompanied by an exhilarated Matty all flushed cheeks and wide eyes. In his enthusiasm Matty awaited no instruction but merely leapt into the boat and positioned himself beside Morven. As he opened his mouth as if to speak, Nunca caught his eye and placed a large patterned finger to his lips.

Zabian, all his senses alert to the sounds and the smells of the night, stood on the riverbank keeping watch for the others. Meanwhile, Nunca aided by Choi, was attempting to fit an elaborate leather harness around his expansive torso. Choi gestured for Nunca to squat down so that he could secure the harness across his back, but Nunca deciding otherwise picked Choi up by his shoulders and perched him on a boulder behind him. Choi worked quickly with small nimble fingers as he pulled and tugged at the contraption until he was satisfied with the fit.

"I think it would be a good idea to allow me to breathe," whispered Nunca over his shoulder, feigning shortness of breath.

Choi raised an eyebrow and pulled the harness tighter. Nunca gave a wry smile. "You're so predictable, my little friend," he whispered, as he turned and found Choi's face level with his own. "How do you like the view?"

"Not to my taste," he grinned. "Besides it's too cold up here." He jumped gracefully down from his perch.

Nunca, positioning himself on the narrow bridle path, breathed deeply and filled his mighty lungs with the sharp night air. He leaned forward into the harness, fixing his eyes ahead as he made ready to absorb the weight of his load, and ease his cargo silently down the river towards the open sea.

Jesyka and Aran appeared, gave quick nods of recognition and took their places beside Morven and Matty. No one spoke as Zabian eased the boat gently from its mooring, jumped in and, securing the canvas cover overhead, plunged them all into darkness.

11

By the time Methna entered King Broehain's presence in the Great Hall at Kinfallon, he was slumped in a chair looking with sightless eyes across the great plain to the south. Torpen stood beside the King attempting to offer words of comfort and explanation, as Ferneth, head upon outstretched paws and eyes half closed caught the fading rays of the hazy afternoon sun.

Torpen could not hide his relief on seeing Methna and stepped forward to greet her. "You are most welcome, Methna. Perhaps you know more? I cannot give my Lord any relief – I cannot calm his fears."

Broehain stood, turned away from the pale sunlight and fixed her with watery eyes. "Why was I not told there was a change to their plans? I had a right to know!"

Methna walked across the room, as if drawn towards the sunlight, and turned to face the King as she positioned herself on the sill of the window. "Good day, my Lord. I am sorry for your distress, but it was felt there was a need to be overly cautious."

"How is kidnapping my daughter in the dead of night and dragging her off to the middle of a war being 'overly cautious'?" he demanded.

"Your son was also *kidnapped* – as you put it – does this not equally give you some cause for concern?" Methna asked.

"Indeed, indeed," Broehain protested, "but he is big enough and skilled enough to look after himself." He dropped back into his chair. "There were things that I wished to speak with her about – important things that were not fully explained and should have been."

"Treachery is unfortunately always around us, my Lord, such is the curse of Volger and the weakness of men. To form one plan and implement another is hopefully an aid to their safety."

"And you fear they have been betrayed?" he asked.

"Remember, my Lord, that my own daughter is the one in most danger, for if Volger realises who she is…"

"Torpen knows how we have suffered," interrupted Broehain. "My wife was taken from me four years past and I begin to fear that I am cursed, and now with this devil Volger at my door – can it be God's will that I should suffer so much?"

Ferneth's eyes fluttered and gentle sighs escaped her mouth as she dreamt.

"My Lord, we all suffer, it is part of our human existence and yes it can feel that our joys are short-lived. But for myself, I do not fear God's will. It is man's will – it is Volger's will – that turns my blood cold."

Methna leant forward, attempting to keep Broehain focussed upon her words. "I see how your loss has blighted your life, but you are King of the Northland and you have a duty to your people. Your own personal tragedy will become but one among so many that will befall this nation, if Volger takes possession of your land. Your descendants will never rule here. Not your son, nor your daughter, nor any one of their line. He will wipe your lineage from the face of the earth."

Methna's cheeks grew pink and her words gathered pace. "I know much, my Lord, about personal tragedy, and I

49

know much about fear, for they are a lethal combination which can cause us to fall to our knees in despair when we should be standing. And we must remain standing for the sake of our children. Aran and Jesyka can secure the Northland's future – they possess the courage of youth and the belief that evil must be challenged. It is our place to stand with them, no matter the odds, no matter the cost."

Silence hung in the air as they sat for a few moments, each lost within their own thoughts.

"We were betrayed once before," Methna continued, "and yet we never knew how or by whom. That betrayal cost us our son's life. Volger's assassins believed that my son was the heir, not my daughter." She paused. "Perhaps this was the source of the rumour that the heir was dead."

The muscles in Methna's face tightened, as she pressed her palms together as if in prayer. "And so as they congratulated themselves that the heir of the Northland was no more, we were blessed with the gift of time; time to recruit the guardians, time to train Jesyka in all manner of skills and in doing so secure her survival."

She breathed deeply. "Volger is meticulous in his planning; years in advance he will gather knowledge about his proposed future conquests – learning their ways, studying their history, locating their weaknesses, laying traps and preying on the weak. Fear is Volger's friend – he uses it to paralyse men, women, armies and whole nations. Great and unconditional sacrifice is needed to counter his endless reign of terror and that is what Jesyka and her guardians offer – and your position is not so different – for you too are called to serve as they are. Your nation and your children look to you to stand with them."

Tears tipped from Broehain's eyes. "I can only think that my children and my people find me wanting – I am emasculated by my loss – I am in a prison – I am entombed and yet I breathe still..."

Methna shivered and rose from her seat. The sun had dipped behind the distant hills and the air grew rapidly cooler. She made her way quietly across the room with Torpen shuffling close behind. As she reached the door, Torpen reached out and gently grasped her arm.

"My cousin, Wensele, was taken by Volger's men in the belief that he knew the identity of the heir of the Southland. Needless to say he did not survive. Either way, the heir was tracked down and disposed of." The old man's grip tightened.

Methna placed her soft pale hand over Torpen's gnarled fingers. "My son, Torpen, was only eight years old."

12

Choi, running ahead, reached the open sea and noted the many fishing boats anchored along the water's edge. Nunca was only a little way behind for they had made good time and though the sky was lightening it was not yet dawn and the harbour lay quiet.

Nunca fell to his knees as Choi swiftly released him from his harness and together they moored the boat alongside the others. Nunca stood, straightened his back, and raising his hands to the heavens, stretched his mighty frame as the light breeze caressed and cooled his skin.

Zabian led the way and Choi occupied the rear, as the band of seven moved rapidly and stealthily along the waterfront. Without altering their pace, they turned swiftly at Zabian's instruction and followed his nimble steps up the gangplank of the *Dancing Monkey*.

Captain Quiggs was waiting for them below deck. He was a large jovial man with a heavy black and grey speckled beard and half a dozen thin silver grey plaits hanging from beneath a black battered hat. His clothes gave the impression of past elegance, vibrant blues now faded and threadbare and metal buttons either tarnished, dinted or long gone: a few broken threads revealing where they had once sat.

"You made it," he grinned, showing even but discoloured teeth, "and in good time too." His eyes took in the unusual cut of his passengers as they discarded their outer clothing and stood shoulder to shoulder in the confined space; his gaze finally settling upon Zabian and his boots. Captain Quiggs could not withhold a chuckle. "Now, what manner of man would wear such boots, I ask myself?"

"One who pays well and promptly," offered Zabian.

"Then we can sail as soon as you tell me where you are bound," replied a grinning Captain Quiggs, "and when you fill my palm with the emerald you promised."

"Then cast off, Captain, and head south."

"You jest," declared Captain Quiggs. "Only a fool would travel south..."

"Indeed, my friend, and that is exactly what you have aboard – the most foolhardy bunch you are ever likely to meet. And the emerald," he held out a clenched leather bound fist and, turning it slowly before Captain Quiggs' expectant face, uncurled his fingers to reveal a glorious dark green stone, "will be yours when you set us down at Iola."

Captain Quiggs threw back his head and filled the cabin with raucous laughter. "It was a blessed day when you crossed my threshold, Mr Zabian. I have not met the like of you before and yet I think we understand each other well."

Behind the mirth his eyes hardened. "We could be good for one another, you and I – for if you keep your promise *and* there is more where this came from..." his eyes skipped from the green orb still nestled in Zabian's outstretched palm, to the boots which teased of untold riches, "...you will not find another Captain who sails these seas, to serve you better or more faithfully."

Captain Quiggs caught Matty studying his apparel with some apparent distaste. "You would do well, laddie, not to judge too quickly by appearances – likewise with regard to this old tub," he slapped the side of the *Dancing Monkey* with a large open hand. "When the time comes, judge me and the missus here," he slapped the timbers again, "by what we deliver."

* * * * * *

The *Dancing Monkey* possessed a long and bizarre history, not unlike her current master, Captain Quiggs. The two had become acquainted for the first time five years earlier when Captain Quiggs had acquired the *Dancing Monkey* when his luck at the dice had seen a miraculous and unprecedented turn in his favour.

She was an unassuming vessel, which was much to Captain Quiggs' liking, as he preferred her outwardly to convey a slight air of neglect, just like himself, whilst inside he had lovingly fitted her out with the finest mahogany furniture. The outer tired timbers of her hold were lined with an inner layer of quality seasoned wood, designed to offer the highest level of protection to the various and often spurious cargoes that were frequently uplifted and delivered under cover of darkness.

Captain Quiggs stood now on the upper deck staring out across a gentle sea with the *Dancing Monkey* in full sail, as he harnessed every breath of the fickle breeze. From the lower deck Jesyka and Aran had been watching him for some time; Jesyka marvelling at how long he had held that pose with his hands loosely clasped behind his back and his grey plaits lifting and prancing in the air.

"Morven is too quiet, Aran," she said, with searching eyes. "She is much changed. Nunca said that she asked no questions and gave no resistance, and not once has she challenged our decision to leave Kinfallon with no word to your father."

Aran sighed. "Morven's moods are a mystery to me. I am as bewildered as you. In my life I have never seen my sister like this." He hesitated. "Well, not that is since the death of our mother."

Jesyka was becoming increasingly frustrated by Morven's unexplained subdued behaviour, but sought to convey none of this as she spoke. "As you know, we sent Nunca believing that she would hiss and spit like a wildcat and knowing that only he had the strength and the gentleness to appease her – and yet she came like a lamb."

When Aran offered no immediate response, Jesyka lifted her face to the sky and, closing her eyes, felt the first few drops of rain.

"My father is but a shadow of the man he was before my mother's death," said Aran. "I believed him to be neglectful of his duty thereafter. I was critical, and Morven was supportive. As time went on he began to lean on her all the more."

Jesyka found herself smiling; enjoying the cool rain as it danced upon her eyelids. "What is it about daughters and fathers? For I dote on my father also."

The smile however was short-lived, as knots formed and tightened in her stomach, and a shiver scurried along her spine. "He was due home in the spring, but we have had no word this past six months..." Her voice trailed away as absentmindedly her grip upon the bulwark grew.

Matty appeared on deck, and steadying himself for a moment, as the strengthening wind caused the *Dancing Monkey* to lurch forward, made his way across the open deck to join them.

"Morven is asking to speak with you again, Aran." The rising wind ruffled his golden curls and he grabbed at the slippery bulwark. "She is distracted," he said despondently, "has eaten little since we left Kinfallon and drunk hardly more. But I cannot get one word of explanation from her."

Jesyka watched as they gripped each other by the forearms and pulled one another close. She felt her heart stir at this outward show of affection: together with a flash of irritation towards the source of their disquiet. Aran slowly released Matty's arms, and turning away staggered ungraciously across the rolling deck, eventually grabbing at the swinging door and disappearing below deck.

"He doesn't look all that seaworthy, does he?" offered Jesyka.

Matty held a faint smile but made no response, and an awkward silence grew and lingered as the sky began to darken. More than once she sensed that he was about to speak, noting that his mouth appeared to open and close like a fish taking in air, but no words came and they watched together as white foam began to form on the tops of the heightening waves.

Eventually, behind her wind tossed hair, Jesyka realised that Matty's clear blue eyes were watching her. "I...I had wanted a moment with you," he began, his cheeks reddening. Jesyka caught at her tresses, spun them expertly in her hand and knotting them at the base of her neck turned to meet his handsome flushed face.

"I doubted Aran's belief in you," he continued, catching at his own unruly locks. "At first, that is – but not now. I know that Torpen speaks endlessly about you being the 'heir' the 'one' – and that this is your destiny, but you always had a choice. And now you are here, the four of you, risking your lives to help us – you could have left and saved yourselves and yet you chose to stay..."

"God curse me for a liar!" boomed Captain Quiggs excitedly, jabbing at the air with a pointed finger and outstretched arm. "But I believe that to be the cliffs of Iola."

13

Volger stared down into the glowing embers of a well-laden fire, as he pushed a smouldering stray log with the toe of his boot back towards the main body of the blaze. The room was warm and the dominance of red in the large floral tapestries that hung upon the walls added to the sense of comfort. As Kamron entered the room, Volger turned from the fire, an uncommonly pink tinge upon his cheeks.

"Well?" he enquired.

"The prisoners are rehoused in the cellars of the Abbey, as you instructed," Kamron responded.

"I take it their journey was suitably arduous?" Volger asked.

"I believe so," Kamron replied, standing now beside his father and shaking his wet cloak before the fire, which hissed in protest.

"And what of the supply waggons?"

"They have been sighted some two miles off." Kamron dropped into a richly upholstered chair close by the hearth and began to pull at his sodden boots. "The roads are not so fine here; the journey was slower than anticipated."

Volger frowned, returning his gaze to the fire and toying again with the log which refused to stay put. "I am impatient to get things settled here. I want food parcels ready for distribution by the break of day."

Kamron leant back in the chair and met his father's intense stare. "The men are exhausted, father," he stated wearily.

"You think me a hard taskmaster, Kamron. But you will learn that to command a force such as this: comprised of miscreants, murderers and the resentful conquered, requires one vital ingredient: absolute discipline." Volger moved away from the fire and began to pace about the room.

"Such discipline must deliver total obedience to my rule; swift punishment for those who fail to adhere and, for my part, the discipline to reward well. This consistency is all that holds this immense disparate fighting force together; for they will walk the length and breadth of any country at my will, once they witness that obedience to me is always generously rewarded."

Kamron threw his boots aside and stretched out his legs towards the heat as Volger continued. "Men are not as noble as they like to think," he scoffed. "One day I can kill a man's kinsman, the next day I can feed whatever family he has left, and the day after that will see him succumb to my will. He will enslave himself to my command to ensure the survival of himself and what is left of his line. Such is the brutal truth of the weakness of men."

He leant upon the back of Kamron's chair and allowed a tentative smile to creep along the thin lips. "I have seen it, over and over: supposedly strong, principled men and women crumble in the face of a force that shows no mercy." A harsh laugh escaped him. "And then they can live out their small lives in peace; for as Supreme Leader *my* will shall prevail and *my* laws will provide order and stability." He stood tall and closing his eyes momentarily rolled his head first to the left and then the right. "And in due course," he sneered, "when we have conquered this Great Crossland and harnessed its abundant riches," he breathed deeply and slowly opened his eyes, "they may even love me for it."

Kamron smirked. "But, father, there is still much to do, for one nation remains unconquered and already the winter snow begins to gather on the northern hills."

Volger returned to stand awhile by the hearth, staring with wide eyes at the dancing flames. The warmth within the chamber cajoled Kamron towards the promise of sleep, as his eyelids grew heavy and his chin soon lay upon his chest.

"The Northland would no doubt have been a formidable challenge," said Volger, unaware that his son now slept, "had we not been so diligent in our forward planning." He smiled as the same wayward log, much reduced in size, once more made a bid for freedom: scattering sparks across his boots as it rolled away. He stamped upon it, crushing the brittle charred wood to nothing more than smoking cinders. "All is in place to deliver a smooth transition of power. I do not anticipate any problems."

PART TWO:
REVELATION

14

It was early evening and the rain was persistent and heavy as Captain Quiggs, assisted by a squally breeze, brought the *Dancing Monkey* stealthily alongside the more southern of the two Iola jetties. The band of seven crouched together on the lower deck, each wearing dark hooded cloaks and facecloths.

Choi was the first to make a move, as he crept, cat-like, onto the top of the bulwark which ran around the perimeter of the lower deck. He perched there on all fours, his eyes fixed on the rain-drenched jetty, as the ship drew closer to its destination. With the *Dancing Monkey* still a ship's length from its intended mooring, Choi leapt, clearing the dark forbidding water with ease and creating nothing more than a gentle splash as he landed upon the water-logged stone.

"Dear Lord, I do believe I've seen it all now," said Captain Quiggs with a shake of his head.

"He likes to entertain," said Nunca, grinning behind his mask as he bent to gather up the heavy mooring line and cast it out towards the jetty.

Choi caught the rope, wrapped it around his waist, threaded it through the nearest rusty iron mooring ring and pulled. Jesyka was next, climbing up onto the bulwark and running at speed down the length of the taut rope with Nunca close at her heels. The three eased the *Dancing Monkey* closer into the side, as Captain Quiggs, signalling for the gangplank to be made ready, waited for the familiar creak of the timbers as the *Dancing Monkey's* sodden rope fenders nestled into the jetty wall.

As the last to disembark, Zabian offered his outstretched hand to the Captain, who grasped it heartily within his own. A smile spread across Captain Quiggs' face that grew so large that his eyes were lost amid folds of skin, as he felt the emerald hard against his palm.

"I like how you do business, Mr Zabian," beamed the Captain.

"Likewise, Captain Quiggs," said Zabian, releasing his hand. "And remember: if you do not receive our signal within three days then leave these waters and look to yourself – for you will have fulfilled your promise to us."

Zabian's eyes crinkled at the corners, as his mask withheld a grin. "But I remain hopeful, my friend, that our paths will cross again very soon."

* * * * * *

The long wide jetty appeared deserted, apart from piles of discarded rope and old sailcloth scattered here and there down its length. Nunca led the way as they moved quickly and silently towards the land. They clambered up the short slipway and along the eerily quiet cobbled street that led directly to the base of the ancient stone staircase.

On reaching the foot of the Abbey steps, Jesyka noticed a small terraced house whose front door had been battered mercilessly: its splintered remains swinging despondently in mid-air. Nunca entered first with the others close behind, as they found themselves in a tiny sparse living area, where a well-worn ragdoll occupied a stool in the corner.

"So Volger's men are already here," said Zabian, loosening the cloth about his face and shaking the water from his cloak. "They have moved at great speed to reach the coast in so short a time, which suggests they have met with little resistance along the way."

"Why have you brought us here to this Abbey?" asked Aran, rubbing his chilled limbs as he paced the floor.

"From past experience of Volger's methods, it was not difficult to surmise that taking this renowned sacred site would be symbolic in convincing an already conquered people that all is lost," offered Zabian.

"Also," added Nunca, "Volger would undoubtedly use the Abbey as his main base. From here he is able to command everything out at sea and across the land for miles in every direction."

"We should explain that we possess knowledge of the Eastland from happier times," said Choi. "This Abbey was the gathering place of all four Kings, when an attempt was made to form an alliance."

"An alliance?" queried Aran. "I have never heard of such a gathering."

Choi settled himself on the floor before responding. "Probably because the alliance never happened. The Kings could not, or more to the point, would not, agree terms whereby each would aid the other should an outside aggressor attack the Great Crossland."

Aran's legs suddenly felt weak and he slumped to sit beside Choi. "Did my father attend?"

"He did," confirmed Choi, "and was vehemently against the alliance."

"But, if you also attended this gathering, why did my father not recognise you?" asked Aran, pushing cold fingers through his thick damp hair.

"We were but three among many who came to witness this historic meeting. It was not difficult to remain anonymous within the shadows."

Aran stared across the room at Morven, who did not raise her head to meet his troubled face. "Morven, did you know about this?"

She made no response, other than to shake her head.

"Have you lost the power of speech?" he asked sharply.

"Aran," Choi reached out and placed his small open hand upon Aran's chest. "We must all rest awhile now. There will be time enough to discuss such matters when this is over."

A welcome heat immediately entered Aran's chest and swept swiftly through his body: alleviating the discomfort of damp clothes and aching limbs. He opened his mouth as if to speak, but his mind was now at ease and no words came.

They spent many hours in quietness, settling themselves upon the floor around the edge of the room. They changed places periodically throughout the night, as they took it in turns to keep watch and wait for a darker sky.

Two hours before dawn, Zabian, on the final watch lifted the cloth to cover his face. The sky had finally descended to a dull matt black as a blanket of rain-filled clouds continued to pour its contents onto the earth below. "I think it's time we made a move," he said.

"We would probably do well to split into two groups for the climb. If either group encounters trouble send the signal," Jesyka said. "And remember to practise what you preach," she added, glancing in turn at each of her guardians; who chose not to meet her gaze. "No heroics."

* * * * * *

Nunca, Zabian and Aran took the direct route up to the Abbey by the centuries old two hundred stone steps. Nunca, keeping to the right, covered the steps two at a time, glancing occasionally over the edge and noting the steep drop to the road below: known locally as Slow Road. Along this road the horses would transport coffins on the aptly named death waggons up to the top of the hill; to be laid to rest in the wind battered burial yard. These last journeys were notoriously slow as the fierce gradient of the climb determined the need for a long winding road that snaked its way around the hillside.

Zabian and Aran kept to the left as they pushed on through the relentless rain, watching Nunca race ahead of them. They were almost half way up when an elderly couple began to make their way down the steps towards them. The couple appeared unsteady on their feet and held on to one another as they proceeded somewhat hesitantly down the centre of the steps. Nunca crouched in the darkness waiting for them to pass, when six men, clad in scarlet tunics, appeared staggering at the top of the Abbey steps.

Aran felt Zabian's steel grip upon his arm. "Volger's men," he whispered, "a little the worse for making merry."

"Get out of the way!" yelled one of the men, as together they headed at speed down the centre of the steps, driving the couple out towards the edge.

"Hey old man, learn some respect for your betters and stand aside," called another.

"You people should know when you're beaten. Move aside, I say – Move!" shouted a third man, causing the couple to stumble, as he thrust his face towards them.

"Quick, Aran," Zabian signalled for Aran to keep moving. Registering the urgency in his voice, Aran clambered up the steps after him, realising that Zabian knew instinctively that Nunca was about to act. As the old woman clung onto her husband's arm, crying out in alarm as he fell away from her, the man at the rear of the party aimed a kick at her back.

Nunca's hood flew back, releasing his long black hair as he leapt forward, catching the man's foot before it struck, and snapping the ankle with a savage twist. The man screamed wildly, throwing up his arms and plunging headlong down the steps. He knocked three of his company clean off their feet as they tumbled together – cursing and swearing as they fell. The two that remained standing could not control their amusement as they laughed out loud and hurled abuse after them. Unaware of what had just occurred, they waited a while until they could contain their mirth before heading gingerly down the steps after them.

Zabian reached the old woman just in time to fix his hand across her mouth and stop her from crying out in despair, in the belief that her husband had slipped over the edge to certain death.

Nunca was laid at full stretch on the edge of the steps with his right arm extended down towards Slow Road. In his hand he held the old man by the collar, as his thin frail legs paddled frantically in the air. Nunca eased himself up onto his knees hauling the old man back onto the steps and into the arms of his astonished wife.

"God be praised, God be praised," she chanted as she cradled his head.

"Dear Lord, in his mercy…" the old man began; his voice trailing away as his eyes beheld his saviour's dark skin and wild rain-sodden hair.

Zabian grinned and slapped Nunca on the shoulder. "Come friend, that's your good deed for the day," he said, as he offered his hand and pulled Nunca to his feet.

The old couple sat for many minutes in the rain replaying in their minds what had just occurred. It was a miracle, of that they were certain, but they were somewhat unsure whether thanking the Lord was all that appropriate, for their guardian angel that night looked more like the Devil himself.

* * * * * *

The steep grassy hillside leading up to the burial yard proved an arduous climb, in particular for Morven, as the saturated grass caused her to slip repeatedly, churning up mud that clung to her boots and the hem of her cloak.

"Not my finest plan," gasped Jesyka to Choi, as she finally crawled over the brow of the hill. He was waiting there with Morven by his side, whom he had carried on his back up the final third of the ascent.

"Perhaps not," he agreed, with mocking eyes.

She threw herself to the ground and pulling the cloth from her face let the rain pound her flushed cheeks. Matty's head appeared at the edge of the plateau, sheer relief etched upon his features, when suddenly he lost his footing and fell face down into the side of the hill. All three rushed forward and catching hold of his dirt-ridden cloak hauled him up and over the edge. Jesyka struggled to hide her amusement, as the facecloth he had lost on the way up had been replaced by a mask of mud.

The sharp easterly wind blowing in from the sea whistled across the cliff top and began to manoeuvre the rain clouds inland. The Northlanders with hoods pulled low made their way towards the tiny church of St Evron, where a single candle burned in the window. As the dispersing clouds began intermittently to reveal a lighter sky, they were soon aware that they were not the only living souls out amongst the gravestones.

Men, women and children were huddled behind the many and varied burial stones and pyres: using them as effective breakers against the harsh wind. The inhabitants of Iola, having only recently been driven from their homes by Volger's men, remained fearful of attempting to return to their properties too soon. The muffled sounds of quiet sobbing were intermingled with raised vexatious voices, as previously good neighbours squabbled and fought over food and shelter.

"So it begins," muttered Choi under his breath.

As they approached the eastern wall of St Evron's, where they had arranged to meet the others, they could clearly see figures moving.

"It's not them," hissed Choi.

"How do you know?" asked Matty.

"Because we can see them," he replied. "Wait here."

Jesyka and Choi dropped to the damp earth and crawled towards the church.

Matty and Morven watched in wonder at a further demonstration of Choi's unnatural agility, as he scaled the church wall and leapt up onto the roof. Jesyka, with one hand in contact with the wall, disappeared from sight.

"I have nothing, nothing to give you – please leave my daughter – please, I have nothing," pled a fair-haired young woman.

"Well now, my beauty, that's not exactly true is it, I mean you could be a little more friendly like and then you can take your daughter, take the food parcel, and go," came a man's harsh voice.

Jesyka felt the anger clawing at her throat as she told herself to breathe deeply and think rationally. One hefty man with a sandy coloured beard held a small sobbing child under his arm like a sack of potatoes. The girl grasped at the air with arms outstretched and hands that opened and closed in the direction of her mother. A much smaller wiry framed man was holding the slightly built woman by twisting her arm behind her back until she whelped with pain.

Jesyka noted with little surprise that the men bore the gold 'V' on their crimson tunics which marked them as Volger's own.

"Good morning, gentlemen," said Jesyka, as she let her hand drop from the wall and laid her hood across her shoulders.

"Hey, where the hell did she spring from!" exclaimed the big man.

Choi crouched on the roof, listened and waited.

"Well, now then that's a turn up," jeered the smaller man. "Want to join the party do you, dearie? Needing food yourself are you?" He grinned at Jesyka, showing his broken teeth and the hefty man laughed out loud.

"To be honest," said Jesyka, with a shrug, "I'm not particularly hungry, but I think this young woman would greatly benefit from at least two of your food parcels."

"Oh Lord, she's a rich one and make no mistake," said the larger man as he put the complaining child down on the grass. "And are you offering to be friendly like, if we agree to this?"

"Hey, hey – hang on – just a minute…" complained the smaller man still holding on to the young mother as his eyes settled upon Jesyka.

Jesyka feigned a smile. "I think, gentlemen, that we could come to some arrangement."

The two men looked at one another and grinned. As the grip loosened on her arm the young mother wrenched herself away and gathered her child up into her arms. She did not run immediately, perhaps feeling some obligation towards the woman with the amber hair, but on a signal from Jesyka, she hastily grabbed two bulging bags of provisions from the over-laden cart, and fled into the darkness.

Jesyka positioned herself with her back against the church wall, as the two men, appearing now a little unsure of themselves, edged closer.

Jesyka threw open her cloak and the men paused. "The choice of weapon, gentlemen, is yours. Unless, that is, you choose to walk away?"

"What is this?" grunted the big man. "Walk away, walk away – we're not walking anywhere."

"I thought she'd be a tricky one," snarled the smaller man, grinning as he produced a short sword from the scabbard at his side.

Jesyka dropped onto one knee and lowered her head, a horn-handled dagger in each hand. As the men moved in she lunged forward with both arms at full stretch. Their mouths gaped open in disbelief and agony at the searing pain tearing upwards from their thighs. As Jesyka rose to her feet, and they descended to their knees, they were equally unaware of the second pair of blades which transformed the screams forming in their throats to lifeless gurgles.

15

At King Broehain's behest Methna was persuaded to leave her cottage in the forest and move into the castle. It allowed her to see more of the daily life of the King, which she was surprised to find, amounted to very little. Without Morven and Aran around to guide and cajole him into dealing with matters as they arose, he appeared as a man of no consequence: a man who had little sense of duty or pride. She could not help but ponder what sort of man he had been before he lost his beloved Queen Sorcha.

By contrast, Methna found that she particularly enjoyed Torpen's company. He had walked the earth for many a year, long before even her father's time, but there were moments when his enthusiasm and excitement allowed her a glimpse of the younger sorcerer still lurking within his ageing frame.

"You will forgive me, Torpen, will you not, if I ask a pertinent question?" asked Methna, as she stood beside him on the balcony of his chamber looking out over Felden Forest.

"Pertinent you say," he scratched at his sparse grey beard, his eyes alive with amusement.

"Well," Methna smiled, throwing an affectionate glance in his direction. "I truly would not wish to offend you; I look to you now as a friend."

"Oh, flattery," he chuckled, "will, my dear, get you absolutely anything you wish from me."

Methna laughed and, reaching down, patted Ferneth's head.

"Your powers," she paused, "appear to be, well, perhaps a little lacking – and I wondered if this was an age thing? If you don't mind me asking?" Her cheeks reddened a little.

Torpen continued to scratch his beard as his shoulders began to shake and the laughter slowly erupted. "I have outlived my usefulness as a sorcerer tenfold," he said, with a mischievous glint in his eye, "but my stubbornness remains fully intact, I can assure you." He attempted to stand tall. "This final task to find the heir has been my passion for many a year, and was all I had left once King Broehain dismissed my apprentice, Daracha." He sighed. "She spent five good, but wasted years by my side."

Shooing Ferneth before him, Torpen headed indoors to occupy his favourite chair. A meagre fire spluttered in the grate as Methna gently coaxed it back to life and added extra fuel. Ferneth settled across her master's feet and Torpen chuckled again.

"Ferneth has also outlived her usefulness, apart from her most important role as my foot warmer and the most loyal confidante a man could wish for." He smiled and wriggled his toes beneath her soft belly.

"Daracha?" Methna prompted.

"Ah yes, quite a girl," he scratched at his beard again. "Well, it was a difficult time in the royal household, with Sorcha dying so unexpectedly. You see, unfortunately Daracha had been making noises, which, I have to admit, I had taken little notice of. I was, and still am to some extent, a practical sorcerer – but Daracha was a different breed: she was instinctive, appeared to have another dimension to her craft. I use to call it her 'knowing'…" he looked above Methna's head as if searching in the ether for the right word, "she had insight into people's thoughts – not exactly reading their minds but a sense of their intent." His eyes warmed. "Do you know she could spot a liar in action at fifty paces? What a girl, what a gift…"

"Torpen, you said she had been 'making noises' – about what?" asked Methna.

"It was the timing really, most unfortunate," said Torpen, shaking his head. "Just before Sorcha's death, Daracha was complaining of sleepless nights – she had a foreboding that a malevolent force was at work. She spoke of this openly but was unable to be precise." A frown developed on his face, and clasping his hands together, he laid them on his lap, his knuckles white through the paper-thin skin.

"And then, suddenly and inexplicably, Sorcha died and King Broehain from that day took so vehement a hatred towards Daracha concluding that either she could have prevented her death, or that she may have had something to do with it."

Methna's eyes searched the old man's face. "When, Torpen? When was this?"

"Four years past – but this you already know?"

"Yes, but can you be more precise? What was the date of Sorcha's death?"

He was quiet for a time, as Methna watched and waited.

"It was autumn four years past," he finally offered, "the day before the Feast of Phiala. Yes, now I remember, because all the preparations for the great feast were cancelled."

"And where did she go, this Daracha?"

"I do not know, my dear," said Torpen softly. "Why do you ask?"

"Because my son also died four years past, on the day before the Feast of Phiala."

16

"Easy climb was it?" asked Nunca, toying with the tip of his bow.

"You could say that," replied Choi nonchalantly.

"Nothing eventful then?" Nunca probed.

"You could say that," said Choi, gripping his pipe between his teeth and puffing heartily on the damp smoking leaves. "What about you?"

"Nothing really, no heroics of course – just a little skirmish – nothing we couldn't handle." Nunca looked across at Zabian, who lowered his head to conceal a smile.

"Likewise," said Choi, meeting Nunca's eye, "we also had a little skirmish nothing we couldn't handle. No heroics, of course."

Close-by at the back of the tiny church of St Evron, Father Leon, a fair-haired young priest, was in earnest conversation with Jesyka and Aran.

"But you are only seven," gasped Father Leon. "Why have you put yourselves in such danger by coming here?"

He searched their faces with anxious, pale blue eyes and before they could answer he spoke again. "He has threatened the Mother Abbess, you know? Unforgiveable, truly unforgiveable." He stroked his throat with nervous fingers. "But I do not understand what you hope to gain?"

"Father, we are the only nation of the Great Crossland still free from this tyrant," said Aran, "and my father, King Broehain, believes he can broker peace with Volger…"

A harsh, nervous laugh escaped Father Leon, as his hands clutched at the cord around his waist. "With all respect, your father must be out of his mind."

Aran sighed. "I am beginning to believe that this may indeed be true, but our only hope is to convince him that we must fight. There is no other option left to us."

Morven started as if about to speak, but then appeared to think better of it.

Father Leon clutched at Aran's arm and peered into his face, "And does your heir of the Tribe of Skea live?"

"We are hopeful that our heir lives," said Aran hesitantly.

"All is in chaos here; no one seems to know if the heir of the Eastland lives or not. Our King Greschwen was a great man, but a man of peace. He believed the stories of Volger were exaggerated – and, as you now see, we have all paid a heavy price for that."

"Morven," Aran turned to face her, "have you not heard enough, do you need to see more?"

"I – I, really need to see this man. I must see him for myself," she said quietly, keeping her eyes averted.

"So be it," said Jesyka.

"Father, will you allow us to enter the Abbey from your church?" Zabian asked. "We know of a passageway that connects these two places of worship."

"Dear God, how could you know of such a thing?" said Father Leon, rubbing his sweating palms down the sides of his habit.

"We were here some years ago, Father, before your time," said Choi.

"Well, it's actually meant to be just here," he patted the side of the font. "But I have always doubted its existence.

To be honest, I have tried to move the font on a number of occasions, always without success, and began to think that perhaps it was just a tall tale."

Without waiting for the others to respond, Father Leon attempted to demonstrate; he placed both hands upon the edge of the font, spread his fingers wide, gritted his teeth and pushed. The others watched with some amusement as the font held its ground; but the young priest was not to be deterred, as he rolled up his sleeves, cleared his throat and tried again. "As you can see…," he said, breathing deeply from the exertion.

Nunca stepped forward. "Allow me."

Nunca placed his large decorated hands beside those of the pale young priest and on a count of three they pushed.

"You just needed a little help there, Father," said Nunca graciously, as the font lurched forward to reveal a gaping hole at their feet. As Father Leon teetered, open mouthed, on the edge of the chasm, Nunca grabbed hold of his coarsely woven habit and hauled him away.

"Glory – what strength," gasped Father Leon as he was lifted clean off his feet. "Indeed sir, you are a very useful chap to have around."

* * * * * *

Father Leon supplied the Northlanders with three spherical wire baskets densely packed with a peat-based mixture, which when lit gave a slow burning light and a not insignificant amount of heat. The peat mixture was stored in two large barrels at the back of the church and used mainly to fill the four braziers positioned along the cliff edge. When the weather was at its most treacherous and the mist rolled in they were lit to warn of the infamous cliff face and the perilous rocks below.

"I wish you well," said Father Leon, taking Jesyka's hand in his own and shaking it heartily. She smiled deeply, noticing the colour in his soft fleshy cheeks.

Matty swung his basket of light out over the black hole and peered down the steep stone steps. "So, who's first?" he asked gingerly.

17

Balac left Estril Forest in the early hours of the morning. Akir raised her head and cocking it to one side watched as Balac saddled Olran, attached the empty saddle bags, and swung himself up and onto her back. Pulling his cloak tight about him, he set out at a gentle pace for the coast.

It was hours later as the first golden rays of dawn appeared upon the horizon, splitting the sea from the sky, that Balac entered the cobbled streets of Iola and headed towards the Abbey steps. If he achieved nothing else that day he was hopeful of taking possession of twenty-four oak-smoked herring.

The hollow sound of Olran's hooves connecting with the stones jarred against the silence as Balac's skin began to tingle and the hairs on his arms lifted. "I must be mad, I should have stayed away," he muttered under his breath. Olran's ears stood proud and she threw back her head and snorted as if in agreement. He leant forward and stroked her neck. "Steady there, old girl; take it easy."

Balac felt his throat tighten; all the signs were here, he had seen it all before: the uncanny quiet, the scavenging dogs, the streets littered with debris from ransacked houses, but no burning, thankfully no burning here. Whoever was plundering this land wanted this place intact. People were watching him from the shadows, he was certain; they would be wondering was he friend or foe.

"Neither," thought Balac, "just a fool."

A small boy peeped out from one of the houses, met Balac's startled expression, and then ran across the road and disappeared down a side street. Balac found himself smiling; the boy had a strangely defiant but almost jovial air about him and appeared quite indifferent to Balac's presence. He slid from the saddle and led Olran on towards the smokery.

"Dear God," Balac exclaimed, as on approaching Old Cal's door he was met with a gaping hole. There was no sign of Old Cal, just fragments of broken fish lying scattered around the storehouse. The wooden rails from which the fish had hung in their dozens had been forcibly wrenched from the ceiling, smashed until they splintered, and lay now littering the floor at his feet; the devastation suggested the raid had been executed with ferocity and haste. Balac breathed heavily, tethered Olran to the broken door frame and began to gather the larger pieces of fish from the floor.

He was no sooner done than he heard a bell ring out from the small church upon the hill and almost immediately became aware of the faint but distinct beat of men marching. Balac ran outside, untied Olran's reins and gently coaxed her into the shadowy recess at the back of the smokery. He was thankful she appeared not to be offended by the over-powering smell of fish, as he held her face close to his own.

Volger's men began their march down the Slow Road six abreast and twenty rows deep. Balac waited and listened, cursing his luck and his own stupidity.

18

Blackness encased them as they moved on in single file; Zabian led the way, peering into the darkness as he swung his burning basket to and fro. The passageway was airless and damp with the aroma of burning peat their only companion.

"I hate being underground," said Nunca, staying close to Matty who carried the second light.

"It's a place best left to the dead," whispered Matty, his eyes casting upwards towards the cemetery overhead.

"Even then I would hate it. We do not lay our dead beneath the earth to bind them forever to the darkness," replied Nunca sullenly.

They continued in silence until Matty suddenly raised his free hand to cover his nose. "What in God's name is that smell?" he complained.

Zabian refitted his facecloth. "We are approaching the bowels of the Abbey. That is the unmistakable smell of human despair. Mark it well."

Walls of black earth were replaced by those of stone and the faint murmur of human voices could be heard a little way ahead; as torches burned in the distance casting a faint glow that led them on.

Choi stopped. "Here, to the left," he whispered, "this must be the staircase that leads directly to the Chapel."

The fresher air flowing down the staircase caught at the baskets, causing them to blaze anew. "I'm with you," said Nunca.

"Here," said Zabian, handing his light to Aran. "We will see well enough without it."

Zabian nodded to Jesyka and the two of them continued along the passageway as the rest ascended the narrow winding staircase, drawing hungrily at the cool comforting air.

By the time the others had caught up with Nunca he already had the trap door ajar.

"Well," whispered Choi, "what can you see?"

"Cloth, like a giant skirt," he answered, as he leant forward and with the tip of his bow raised the hem but a few inches revealing a shaft of soft warm light.

Morven moved up beside him, noting the richly embroidered fabric and two stone pillars, one to the left and one to the right, supporting a marble slab above their heads.

"We're beneath the altar. The cloth is an altar frontal," she said.

Nunca raised the cloth even higher, revealing an ornate mosaic floor bathed in the golden glow from giant candelabra ablaze upon the altar.

"Visitors from the Northland, welcome to Iola," came a woman's small faltering voice.

Nunca's eyes narrowed and he nodded to Choi who crept from the trapdoor and hid himself in the darkness of one of the stone pillars.

Confused, Aran grabbed Morven's arm in a vice-like grip and pulled her to him.

Nunca, content that Choi was well hidden, turned to the others.

"This is a trap and no mistake," he said softly, "into which we have no option but to walk."

******

Jesyka and Zabian moved on swiftly. As they approached the bars of the first cell they stopped, and crouching low amongst the shadows waited and listened. As Zabian signalled to Jesyka to move forward, a gentle moan escaped from the darkness and held them fast.

"Is someone there?" asked a man's hoarse voice.

Zabian's hand clutched at Jesyka's arm, his eyes wide with horror and disbelief.

Jesyka felt her heart leap and her eyes prick with tears. "Father?" she said softly, pulling the mask from her face and grabbing at the bars with both hands as she glared into the darkness.

"Jesyka, can it be you?" Raghnall's voice was rasping and his breathing laboured. "Or are you just a figment of my crazed imagination…"

"Dear God, father it is me. I am here and Zabian is with me."

"God be praised," said Raghnall.

Zabian produced a knife with a blade no thicker than a meat skewer, disabled the lock and stood aside as Jeyka entered and fell on her knees before her father. As she leant forward to embrace him he shrank away. "No, my love, I would not survive your embrace, my body is too broken."

The dim light hid from Jesyka's eyes the full extent to which Raghnall's body had been disabled by the torturer's skill.

"Oh father, what sorrow to find you so and yet what joy to behold you again," she slid her hand out across the filthy straw and touched the ends of his fingers.

Raghnall gently caressed her hand and sighed. "I was careless. I attempted to travel home through conquered lands, alone and in disguise, in the hope that I might gain some knowledge of Volger's plans for the Northland..." his voice was fading, "...and I had wanted so much to spend one more summer with you and your mother." Jesyka gulped at the stale air as she fought to smother the sobs that grew in her chest.

"Jesyka," his voice took on a graver tone. "I cannot leave this place, you cannot save me. My time is almost at an end."

He tried to raise his hand to ward off any protest, but could lift it no higher than to clutch at her forearm. "You will leave me here in this filth to die because you know you must," he added.

"Father, I am strong. I could carry you on my back, please..." Jesyka pleaded.

Raghnall lifted his eyes towards Zabian.

"It is good to see you again, old friend."

Zabian gave a gentle bow of his head, as he kept watch through clouded eyes.

Raghnall gazed once more into his daughter's face. "You have made it here, my love, into Volger held land, into the very heart of his domain and that is a sign for me that you will succeed." He coughed, wincing at the pain. "I can feel the strength that courses through your very being," his fingers tightened just a little upon her arm, "and my spirit soars to know that our blood, together with those of generations past, are at one in you." Jesyka pressed the back of a trembling hand hard against her mouth, stifling the cry that scratched and clawed to be free.

"You will fulfil your destiny," he gasped, glancing again towards Zabian, "but it will not be easy." The faintest of smiles appeared upon his face. "Your guardians, your mother, they will stand with you for you are the embodiment of hope for our people."

"Yes, father, I know – but against such an enemy as this? Look what he has done to you," she wailed softly.

Jesyka's tears ran freely now as Raghnall continued. "Believe me, Jesyka, when I say that you will never be truly alone – for even when you face your darkest hour, when you are forced to make the most difficult of decisions – always know that I am with you."

Jesyka felt that her heart must surely break as she sobbed.

"Be strong, my beauty," he sighed, "and remember this: think always with the head, so beautiful a head; and listen to the heart, so fierce a heart; and then if still you cannot find the answer reach for the spirit. Let the spirit in and I will speak with you, you will know me again, daughter; though my life here with you is over."

Zabian stepped back into the cell, his eyes still fixed upon the passageway. "Jesyka, we must go, unless it is your will that we all die here this day."

Raghnall smiled weakly and coughed a little. "Indeed, see! Good counsel is all around you, if you will but listen." He paused; his grip upon her arm falling away. "Leave me the dagger…"

"No, father," she gasped. "Dear God, you cannot ask that of me."

"Think," he reasoned. "Think with the mind and listen to the heart. I would not ask this of you if there was any other way… I am sorry for your pain…"

Jesyka's tears left clean tracks through the dirt upon her face as she reached with an unsteady hand for a blade beneath her clothes.

"I do not have the strength to do it myself, my love," his voice was gentle and growing fainter, as he lifted his gaze beyond her. "Perhaps Zabian will oblige an old friend, will he not?"

Jesyka glimpsed a trace of desperation in his face, to be free of this broken body and she knew that she could not deny him this final request.

She bent her head and leaning forward rested it gently against her father's forehead as he closed his eyes.

"Keep me forever in your heart, Jesyka, and I *will* live on."

Rising to her full height she handed the dagger to Zabian who now stood beside her. She stepped away and turned her back, knowing that she would never see his adoring glance, his gentle eyes and his loving face again.

19

The sun assisted by a westerly breeze began to dry the sodden grass of the graveyard and the shiny cobbles grew dull. Balac remained in the shadows until the shouts of the soldiers and the beat of their marching boots had long gone. Olran grew restless and pawed the earth. He could hear other voices now, those of inhabitants, emboldened by the daylight and the warmth of the sun, who began to emerge from their hiding places and drift back towards their homes. They wept at the destruction of their livelihoods, their loss of loved ones, and they conversed in the hushed and bowed tones of a conquered people.

"Who's there?" asked a man, who hovered in the doorway. He waited a few seconds and then, leaning forward, peered into the shadows.

Balac remained silent, but Olran snorted and stamped with impatience.

The man stepped cautiously over the threshold, his eyes adjusting to the darkness.

"Who's there, I say, show yourself?" the voice came again, a little bolder now.

"Is that you, Old Cal?" called Balac softly, leading Olran forward.

"Ah, the stranger who ordered the fish," Old Cal smiled weakly. "Your timing is poor, young man," he offered, giving a resigned shrug.

"This is a sorry sight," said Balac, as he grasped Cal's outstretched hand and shook it heartily.

"All that lies broken here can be repaired given time," said Cal. "But that is not so for the hearts and souls of men."

A thin young boy in ragged clothes suddenly appeared at the entrance. "Cal, they're looking for you, the soldiers," he hissed into the darkness.

Instantly, the boy was shoved aside. "We seek one known as Old Cal," a thickset soldier bellowed into the smokery, filling the void where the boy had stood. Cal, gesturing to Balac to remain in the shadows, stepped forward and back into the sunlight.

"He's here, my Lord, the old dog is here," the soldier called out over his shoulder. Crouching in the darkness, Balac heard the approach of a horse upon the cobbles. He heard the rider dismount and the beat of his boots upon the stone.

"Are you the proprietor?" said Kamron, his nose wrinkling at the overpowering smell of fish, as he peeled off his fine leather gloves. Old Cal nodded.

"How long will it take you to remedy this?" he asked, gesturing towards the chaos within. Balac noted his slim build beneath the sumptuous cloak and the paleness of his skin.

Old Cal shrugged. "Left to my own devices, possibly two or three weeks."

"You have two days," Kamron replied flatly. "You will detail what provisions you require, and how many craftsmen you need, and they will be with you before noon."

Old Cal raised his eyebrows. "And the fish?" he enquired.

"The boats will be out on the next tide. We will ensure that you have fish aplenty, old man." Kamron waved the gloves in front of his nose and turned sharply away.

"Well, well," mused Old Cal, as he stepped back into the shadows. "Would you believe it. They could have saved themselves a heap of trouble if they had refrained from smashing the place to pieces in the first place."

"Not quite business as usual," offered Balac as he led Olran forward again. "But at least they intend to feed the people."

"You would do well to stick around and busy yourself awhile. You'll draw unwelcome attention if you try to leave just now," reasoned the old man, as he bent to retrieve a broken yard brush from the floor.

"Are you handy with a broom?" Cal enquired as he tossed it towards him. Balac caught the broom with both hands, a grin quickly spreading across his face.

20

Back in the passageway Jesyka sat slumped against the stone wall, squeezing her stinging eyes shut in an attempt to stop the flow of burning tears.

"Jesyka," she heard her name. Someone was calling her name. "Jesyka."

"Yes," she whispered; hastily dispersing the tears by dragging an arm across her face. "Yes, I'm here."

Zabian stood on the opposite side of the dim passageway. "Clear your head as best you can." His voice, so familiar, was firm. And as she forced herself to focus on his face, she beheld a haunted glaze upon his eyes, the like of which she had never seen before.

She pressed the back of her head against the wall, placed her hands upon her thighs and felt the muscles burn as she forced herself to stand. Zabian stood armed with a slim two-foot long forked blade of steel in his left hand, and his beloved double-edged scimitar with a cross guard inset with rubies, in his right. She unclasped her cloak and tossed it aside. Reaching over her right shoulder she released the broadsword from its sheath and locking her fingers around its familiar hilt she gestured to Zabian that she was ready.

As the sound of men's voices grew louder, Zabian attempted a smile. "Time we introduced ourselves."

They ran side by side along the narrow passageway, emerging almost at once into an open chamber inhabited by more than two dozen of Volger's men. Jesyka understood that the element of surprise would only afford them an advantage amounting to seconds. A trestle table in the centre of the room was strewn with half eaten plates of food and jugs of ale. Initially the half dozen men still seated at the table appeared frozen to the spot, with open mouths and expressions of incredulity.

Jesyka ran at the table. She leapt forward stepping onto one seated man's thigh, and propelling herself upwards bore the point of the broadsword down into the table top. Keeping both hands connected to the hilt, she somersaulted in an arc over the sturdy blade to land centre stage. With a flick of her wrists she released the sword from its mooring. A roar of defiance erupted from her throat as she swung the tapered double-edged blade into action.

"Nothing like a grand entrance," called Zabian, as he leapt upwards to join her. The soldiers, now roused from their stupor, grabbed any weapon they could find and surrounding the table bore down upon their intruders.

Effortlessly manoeuvring the forked short sword, Zabian repeatedly ensnared the various blades that thrust towards him; a momentary twist wrenching the offending weapons with ease from their owners' grasp and flinging them every which way across the room. His jewel-encrusted boots connected repeatedly with flesh and bone; as bodies, bloodied and groaning, others silent and still began to litter the floor. With the scimitar twirling and slashing through the air, Zabian's eyes searched the frenetic scene for an opportunity to escape, when he noticed in the doorway the appearance of a pale-faced youth, in a cloak of finest brocade. The young man was accompanied by more men, who roared at the spectacle before them and rushed forward to join the fray.

Kamron stared open-mouthed at the sight of Jesyka. Her eyes were clear and wide now, as the pain of Raghnall's death raged within and fed into every blow. She should have been more aware, alert to Zabian's intentions and continually assessing the situation; all of this should have been like second nature, but her heart was ablaze, as she fought on in oblivion.

When Zabian signalled he was about to make a move, she missed it. He leapt from the table and using the heads of four charging soldiers as stepping stones, dropped at Kamron's feet. Before he could even curl his fingers around the hilt of his sword, Kamron felt cold curved steel hard against his throat. Only when the supply of soldiers to fight was exhausted did Jesyka realise her error; the shock instantly cooling the fire within.

"Damn it," she cursed under her breath, her chest heaving with the exertion. She had been too busy breaking heads, too indulgent of her own emotions. "Damn it," she screamed out. Her heart raced, but her blood ran cold. She stood alone on the table top as the few soldiers who remained standing backed away: their eyes fixed upon Kamron.

Jesyka jumped from the table and moved to Zabian's side. "I'm sorry," she whispered avoiding his eyes. There were groans from the bodies that littered the floor as the wounded began to rise to their feet. But they kept their distance.

"Let's go," said Zabian in Kamron's ear, pushing him forward and away from the chamber towards a wide flight of stone steps that climbed steeply before them. Glancing back over her shoulder, Jesyka noticed the horror on the faces of the soldiers and realised that this young man was someone of great importance. Zabian hesitated at the unmistakable sound of many boots pounding down the steps towards them.

Jesyka could not withhold an anguished sigh. "I'm sorry, Zabian," she offered again, as the knot in her stomach tightened and all she wanted to do was cry: tears for Raghnall, tears for Methna and tears of shame for herself.

Kamron spoke to Zabian, though his eyes remained on Jesyka. "You cannot escape. My father would never allow it."

Jesyka turned to look at the gaunt young man with the blade at his throat and noticed there was no fear in his eyes. He smiled at her and the rage within her reignited.

"You may be right," Zabian replied. "But God loves a trier – so they say."

* * * * * *

Zabian kept his eyes focussed upon the steps as they were overrun by soldiers: an ever-growing sea of crimson forming in front of them. He stepped back, pressing the blade a little deeper into Kamron's flesh. Jesyka positioned herself back to back with Zabian, holding the broadsword out in front of her, as the walking wounded closed in from behind.

"Zabian," she whispered. "Tell me you've been in worse scrapes than this."

"If I could think of one, I would," he replied, a twitch upon his lips.

"Stand aside, stand aside," screamed a voice, as the waves of crimson parted and Volger burst through. When he saw his son, he halted. His breath catching in his throat as his frame grew rigid with fury. Beads of sweat sprang to life upon the polished skull as he thrust out his lower jaw and glared at Zabian.

"Release my son!" he bellowed.

"Father, they were magnificent…" Kamron could not hide the admiration in his voice or the flush upon his cheeks, "together they overcame more than thirty men."

Volger's eyes studied Zabian, the weapons, the clothes, the boots. "I know you," he hissed, his face becoming more animated.

"I believe we have met," offered Zabian.

Volger raised his arm and called over his shoulder. "Bring the prisoner forward."

Jesyka's heart plummeted. She lowered her sword and turned to watch as the crimson sea parted for a second time, and Morven, in her velvet jacket of peacock blue, was thrust into view.

"Oh, no," Jesyka mouthed softly.

"As I said, *Zabian*…" Volger spoke, his thin lips quivering, recognition in his eyes, "…release my son."

21

Balac pondered Old Cal's offer to stick around and help restore the smokery to its former glory; however as the day lengthened and more craftsmen gathered, he began to grow uneasy. He said little and tried not to draw attention to himself but was aware that one of the assigned carpenter's daughters had taken rather a fancy to him. Her father had ordered her home, but she stood a little way off with a girlfriend who was as tall as she was round: whispering and watching. This was amusing many who gathered at the site, including Old Cal, but not the girl's father, who glared continually from beneath heavy, dusty eyebrows.

The two young girls became three and then four, as word of the tall handsome stranger with green eyes and sandy coloured hair spread. Obviously, Balac reasoned, they all knew he was not from these parts and felt certain that it would only be a matter of time before the toothless carpenter became so incensed that he would point him out to one of Volger's men.

"I can remember the day, oh long time ago now, when I could turn a young girl's head," said Old Cal with smiling eyes, as he offered Balac a ladle of fresh water.

Balac rolled his eyes heavenward and sighed.

"However," continued Cal, "on this occasion it is more than inconvenient. I think we need to get you out of here.

Your handsome face could be the death of you."

Balac bent forward to accept the ladle. "And what do you suggest?" he whispered.

"I overheard the guards earlier. There's to be some sort of gathering up at the Abbey within the hour, and many have been ordered to attend," said Cal. "They intend to leave only one man to oversee the work here. We can easily distract just one. Who knows, perhaps the young ladies will oblige." He chuckled softly. "In the meantime, I will keep Olran out of sight and see that she is packed and ready to go."

Balac grasped the old man's arm as he turned to move on. "You are a good man, Cal," he said in earnest, "and I thank you."

"Come and knock upon my door again, young man, in better times," said Cal, raising his head to meet Balac's clear bright eyes. "This madness cannot last forever." He stifled a sigh and forced a grin. "And then we will gorge ourselves on the finest fish, washed down with a barrel of mead."

22

Aran struggled to order his thoughts.

He sat by the window in a chamber high within the Abbey looking out over the cliffs to the flat grey sea beyond. Though they were prisoners, they were not bound, and the room which held them was well furnished. Having been relieved of all their weaponry, the six had been herded into the chamber and the door securely locked and bolted.

Aran watched as the gulls, gently buffeted by the changing currents of air, hovered with wings outstretched, to and fro, in and out, over the cliff edge. He tried to remember all that had been said, in the hope that his brain would eventually make sense of it all; for as yet he remained numb, appearing devoid of all emotion in response to what he now knew.

He glanced across the room at his sister, the ever-faithful Matty by her side, and recalled the moment when the key had turned in the lock behind them and Morven, with ashen skin and fearful eyes, told of their father's betrayal.

Following the meeting at the cottage in Felden Forest, King Broehain had confided in Morven that he had entered into a pact with Volger, years earlier, whereby he would endorse him as Supreme Ruler of the four nations of the Great Crossland. Her distress on hearing this news had caused her father to cut short his confession, suggesting that they should discuss this further the following day: promising that once she was aware of all the facts, she would, at the very least, understand why he had chosen to acquiesce. However, before dawn broke the next day Morven was already heading south. So this, thought Aran, was the knowledge she had been wrestling with; finally deciding to tell no one until she had met Volger for herself and discovered why her father had agreed to surrender their homeland without a fight.

Jesyka had stared at Morven in disbelief. "And you did not think fit to share this information with *us*?"

"I hoped that perhaps I could talk with Volger…" Morven had offered weakly. "That perhaps I could…"

"*That you could talk with Volger*," Jesyka had spat out the words. "That he would indulge you in a cosy chat by the fireside, and you would politely ask for your country back! *Are you insane?*" she had roared.

Aran remembered how Zabian had placed a hand firmly upon Jesyka's shoulder and rooted her to the spot.

"It is of no consequence now," he had spoken slowly, and looking down at Jesyka had waited for her to meet his gaze. "Nothing could have altered what happened to Raghnall."

As Zabian told of the circumstance of Raghnall's death, Nunca had taken himself off to the farthest corner of the room, released the red and black blanket from his shoulder and spreading it out had settled himself cross-legged upon the floor. Within seconds his eyes had closed, a quiet hum emanating from still lips, as his great torso gently rocked to and fro.

Aran sucked hard at the air as he recalled how Jesyka had allowed Zabian to fold her in his arms as she sobbed; for, more than anything, he had wanted to be the one to comfort her.

* * * * * *

As the bolts were thrown back and the key turned in the lock, Zabian was the first to his feet. "Whatever greets us beyond that door, we must work together now as one," he urged, "and trust that Choi will find a way…"

Their hands were bound tightly in front of them, with heavy twisted black rope that tore at the skin. A length of the rope was left to hang from their bindings and trail upon the floor, as they were led out of the high chamber and down a seemingly endless winding staircase until they reached ground level. Directly ahead was a tall arched door, some forty feet high, which swung open at their approach to reveal a cavernous hall within.

They entered down a central walkway with row upon row of Volger's men crowded into the vast space. The majority were clothed in the now familiar crimson with the emboldened golden V upon the right shoulder: but others wore their own colours. These men, still clothed in the livery of their recently burnt and conquered lands, fought now for Volger, to ensure the safety of their kin back home. They watched with curious eyes as the band of six were paraded amongst them.

"Ever the thespian," murmured Zabian, as he surveyed the scene.

Though it was daylight still, the light was poor and Volger, desiring to create a memorable spectacle, had ordered torches to be lit throughout the hall and two glowing braziers, each the height of a man, framed the raised platform upon which Volger and Kamron now stood.

"Welcome, men and women of the Northland," Volger opened his arms wide, grinned broadly, and inclining his head slightly beckoned the guards to deliver the prisoners onto the platform. "You will pardon my manners but you are, what shall we say, an unknown quantity."

Jesyka felt her pulse begin to rise. She bowed her head, averting her eyes from Kamron's intense stare and willed herself to remain calm as she complied with the tug upon the rope. "And therefore," he continued, "I cannot let you remain unfettered."

Six rings of steel were fixed to the wooden floor on which they stood; as one by one they were led forward and securely tethered. Volger could barely contain his joy. He strode, resplendently dressed in black fur, with his hands behind his back, head held high, and surveyed his prisoners.

"Let me introduce our unexpected visitors," he began, standing before Aran at the far left of the stage. "Here we have young Lord Aran, heir to the Northland," he paused. "Well, he was, but his father in his wisdom has agreed to hand over sovereignty to me and..." Aran opened his mouth to protest, but with a lightening blow Volger whipped the back of his hand across Aran's face. "Naughty, naughty," he scolded. "So many of the privileged young have no manners, no manners at all."

Blood trickled from the lacerations on Aran's face and seeped in at the corner of his mouth. Stunned, he shook his head and yanked on the rope, as a roar of pure rage erupted from his throat. Volger smirked, looking down as the back of his hand and the metal studs soiled with blood.

"Moving swiftly on," he said, turning his gaze upon Morven. "Now this, if I am not mistaken, is the lovely Lady Morven. A real beauty, just like her dear departed mother."

Morven bit her lip, her fingers curling to form small delicate fists. Volger raised his hand. Instinctively she squeezed her eyes shut, the tears oozing out between thick lashes, as he merely patted her cheek. "There, there," he mocked; glancing back with a satisfied smirk, as he beheld Aran's bloodied and horrified expression. "I have a surprise for you both," he said. "Come, come, Lady Morven, open those pretty eyes. You'll not want to miss this."

Through the arched doorway came two thick-set men, each bearing a heavy chain attached to a steel cage which they dragged into view. Their burden crept forward on uneven wheels that scraped and screeched upon the tiled floor. At first sight the cage appeared to be empty, but Jesyka could see that those who turned to look upon the cage quickly averted their eyes.

Volger breathed deeply puffing out his chest as the cage continued down the aisle. "If you have not already worked it out, there were two reasons why your father agreed to a peaceful handover of the Northland. One, which must by now be common knowledge, is the unfortunate – for you, that is – death of the Northland's heir of the Tribe of Skea: Jaclan, son of Raghnall – a charming boy by all accounts." He paused. "And the second…"

When the vehicle finally creaked to a halt before the stage the silence was audible; until the two men, easing the hefty chains from their shoulders, allowed them to clatter to the floor. A creature, in lice-ridden rags, was slumped in the corner. It bore a skeletal face of pure white, hollow eyes and nothing more than tufts of matted dark hair, as it stared up towards the glowing braziers. The creature appeared entranced by the abundant light and grabbed repeatedly at the bars with long bony fingers tipped with curled blackened nails. Persistence was finally rewarded as it raised itself from the floor. The light revealed angry sores upon the creature's lips which cracked open, as a grimace revealed darkened teeth.

"Come, come, children," Volger roared. "This is no way to greet your long lost *mother*." He laughed. "Let me present the delectable Queen Sorcha."

Jesyka gasped, her throat constricting as if a mighty hand closed around it and her skin crawled at the horror of

Volger's words. A sickening scream akin to that of a wounded beast burst from Morven, as her legs gave way. Tears burst from terror-stricken eyes as she stared in disbelief at the creature in the cage; whose head turning towards the noise, gazed blankly up at her. Morven wailed upwards to the vaulted heavens, her fingers clawing at the rope that bound her; as Aran watched, his face a bloodied, contorted mass of pain.

"And now," Volger lifted the hem of his cloak and stepped dismissively over Morven, prostrate upon the floor. "Whilst the youngsters gather their wits about them, let me introduce you to the star attractions: Zabian, a true prince of the desert lands and Nunca, Chief of the Wacaaki."

As he fanned out his cloak behind him, he lunged forward and standing on tiptoe stared upwards towards Nunca's face. "Why, I ask myself. Why, do you come to join the Northlanders against me?" he hissed. "Your tribe lives many leagues from here across the great Ancean Sea and yet you choose to come here to make war with me?"

Jesyka, leaning forward, could see Volger's hand toying with the hilt of a dagger, as his agitation grew. "Far better you had stayed home, hunting the hump-backed beasts that I am told roam your endless plains." He snatched the dagger from its sheath. "But no, you come to creep about with your friends here, to hunt me. Why?" He stamped upon the rope that held Nunca to the ring and brought him crashing to his knees. Volger's head gave a slight twitch, a smile of satisfaction upon his lips, as he waited.

"Oooooh, the strong silent type," he said, the flush upon his neck beginning to spread as his skin grew damp. "I would have expected nothing less. What I would give to have ten men such as you in my ranks."

He held the blade upright in front of Nunca's expressionless face and swung it repeatedly from left to right, clicking with his tongue to the rhythm of the swinging blade. Nunca, looking beyond the blade and Volger's crazed features, detected a slight movement overhead. Jesyka had also seen it, but gave no outward sign, aware that she remained the sole focus of Kamron's scrutiny.

"I believe that you are only too well aware of why we came," said Zabian, his words ringing out through the hall.

Volger's nostrils flared and the clicking stopped. "Indeed, Zabian, is that so," his eyes widened. "I was coming to you… But perhaps you are impatient for my attention."

The blade hung in Volger's hand as he suddenly turned his back upon Nunca and glared out into the crowd. His menacing unpredictability cast a chilling shadow, as Jesyka witnessed countless expressions of unease and others of pure undisguised fear.

He walked down the steps and raising the dagger, halted by the cage. Again Aran strained against the rope, but to no effect, other than to shred the skin about his wrists. Volger ran the blade sharply across the bars, causing Sorcha to cry out in alarm, and throwing back his head delivered a triumphant manic laugh as he strode down the central aisle towards the back of the hall. As Kamron turned to watch his father, Jesyka scanned the ornately carved ledges that decorated the top of each supporting stone pillar and saw him. He crept in the shadows beyond the blaze of the torches, leaping from ledge to ledge as he made his way steadily onwards towards the platform.

"He's here," she whispered to Matty, "Choi."

Matty raised his head, "Where?" he asked.

"Everywhere," she replied, a flush suddenly coursing her face, as she felt Kamron's gaze once more.

Volger stopped just short of the arched doorway, turned, replaced the dagger in its sheath and took up his earlier pose: head high, hands behind his back. He lifted his chin and narrowing his eyes, began with steady even steps to make his way back towards the platform.

"So, Zabian, enlighten us all," he boomed. "You have an attentive audience, entertain us."

"We came to show Lady Morven the nature of the beast named Volger," he paused. "And you have not disappointed. You have shown your multi-faceted depravity in abundance."

Volger stopped. Audible gasps rippled amongst the throng as Volger began to clap with a slow steady beat, a sneer quivering to life upon his face. "Brave words," he called, his breath growing shallow. "Brave words indeed, from an army of six!" His head gave an involuntary twitch. "But why?" he continued. "This is the question that is not answered. Why would the likes of Zabian and Nunca, trouble themselves…"

"And Raghnall…" Jesyka called out.

Volger's head swung towards the far end of the stage and for the first time, he considered the girl. "Ah, interesting," he tapped a gloved finger against his lips, a slight frown upon his forehead.

"And what do you know of the *Great*," he mocked, "Raghnall?"

"That he has been tortured mercilessly at your will, and that his corpse now lies in the cellars of this Abbey." Jesyka's voice was steady as she felt all the loathing and vile contempt that she held for this man surge through her blood.

"His *corpse*," Volger sniggered. "I will break him before he dies, I will make him talk and I will know his purpose and I will know yours." Volger wiped the dampness from his forehead with the palm of his glove. He grabbed at the nearest man. "Go to the cellars and bring me news of Raghnall."

Jesyka waited, until all eyes were upon her. "I see you have an impressive army at your command," she began.

"The colours and the ancient symbols of all three sister-lands of the Northland are present here: the black of the Southland with the majestic silver-backed eagle," Jesyka gestured out towards the crowd with her bound hands, "the green of the Westland and the tenacious long-tusked boar, and the blue of the Eastland with the mighty grey wolf." The men who wore these colours grew uneasy, some cursing under their breath. Her tone darkened. "You bring dishonour upon your native colours and shame upon your ancient symbols to bear them here," she paused. "Far better that you wore the crimson, for that is indeed what you have become, Volger's own."

"We had no choice," called out a fresh-faced youth indignantly, as he thumped at the image of the boar displayed upon his breast.

"There is always a choice, my friend," added Zabian. "I think you chose badly."

"And the brown," called out another from the crowd, "the brown of the Northland and the great stag will soon stand here beside us." Volger smirked at this retort, as murmurs of agreement rippled through the hall.

"That, I can promise you, will never happen," said Jesyka, as she shook her amber hair defiantly and strained against the black rope to stand as tall as she could. "For the pact with King Broehain is void; Volger has reneged on its terms. He has treated his royal hostage, Queen Sorcha, with contempt…" on hearing her name, Sorcha lifted her head and turned to stare at Jesyka: distress growing in her eyes. "And…" Jesyka attempted to continue.

"*Who are you?*" screamed Volger, jabbing a pointed finger at Jesyka, as the man returning from the cellar whispered into his ear. Volger's lower jaw jutted forward, his features gradually distorting, as blood rushed anew into his face.

Jesyka saw his discomfort, her heart lifted and her voice grew ever bolder. "I am one who would say to all of you here this day, that when you have lost everything, then you must fight even harder. Then you must hold true to that which you know to be right." Her eyes began to prick with tears, as she felt the beat of her heart strengthen, and she knew that Raghnall was with her.

"I know that Volger's promise of peace is tempting: no more fighting, no more dying, no more burning. But this is a man without honour, without courage and without mercy. The price of his peace is too high." She reached out straining against her bonds towards Volger. "And how will you explain to your children, and your children's children, that you swore allegiance to *this*."

With everyone's attention on Jesyka as she spoke, Nunca having remained on his knees, strained against the iron ring that bound him and finally heard the wood begin to crack.

"We of the Northland cannot live with Volger's peace," she continued, "where a man has no will of his own, no choice and no freedom. He will crush every ounce of spirit that you possess. He will demand your very soul and he will take you – and your kin – to the depths of despair." Jesyka looked down at her hands, transformed now into shaking fists with knuckles as white as death.

Kamron's anxious eyes stared out across the floor towards his father, who stood, head in hands, screaming for silence against the babble of many voices.

"*What is your name? I demand to know your name*," Volger screamed again in frustration, as he marched back towards the platform, his blazing eyes fixed upon Jesyka.

She glanced upwards and on the signal from Choi, she roared back defiantly. "Your pact with King Broehain is also void because the heir of the Northland lives! My name is Jesyka. I am the daughter of Raghnall and Methna and *I* am the Northland's heir of the Tribe of Skea."

* * * * * *

The hall erupted with a cacophony of men jeering, others cheering and the raucous clash of weapons. Volger fuelled with outrage and disbelief, slipped on the steps leading up to the platform, the dagger flying from his hand. "Kill the girl! Kill the girl!" he screeched, spittle flying from his trembling lips.

Only a handful of his warriors heard his cries above the clamour, as Kamron, ignoring the tethered Northlanders ran across the platform towards his father. "No," he yelled, fear etched into his twisted young face. "No, father. Not the girl!"

Roaring with the effort, Nunca finally wrenched the metal ring, still attached to a length of splintered wood, free from the floor in front of him. He jumped to his feet and swung the newly formed weapon into the side of Kamron's head. The impact lifted him off his feet and threw him spread-eagled against the brazier, which swayed precariously for a moment before pitching forward and spewing its glowing contents out into the crowd.

Screams lacerated the air, as Choi leapt from the stone ledge and landing at Jesyka's feet, released the load strapped to his back. The confiscated weapons spilled out across the stage and a mighty grin grew across Nunca's face as he beheld the bow and sheath of arrows at his feet.

"Hey, little friend," he called, "it is good to see you."

Choi swiftly cut the others free from their bonds as Nunca, continuing to swing the hefty missile, defended the stage from the men in crimson. With one final swoop he dropped the weight onto the roof of the cage, causing the bars to buckle and the door to fall from its rusty hinges. As Sorcha crawled towards freedom, she watched wide-eyed as Volger scuttled away beneath the stage and disappeared from view.

Nunca ripped iron bars from the cage and threw them to Aran and Matty, who leaping down, swung them around like madmen holding Volger's men at bay; as Nunca, gathering Sorcha into his blanket, lifted the almost weightless body gently from its prison.

Jesyka, fully re-armed, remained upon the stage loosing arrow after arrow at the crimson foe. From there she could see the chaos in all its glory. As the fire grew bolder and the flames leapt higher, men abandoned battling with their neighbours and turned to flee the greater enemy. In the panic, stronger bodies knocked the weaker to the ground; trampling them underfoot as they pushed forward, eyes fixed blindly ahead: none wanting to witness the carnage beneath their feet.

"This way, follow me," called Choi, as he led the Northlanders away from the madness towards the back of the hall. Ingeniously hidden within the shadow of a stone carved recess was a narrow door. Choi banged with his fist twice. The door swung open and they were instantly moving along a dark airless passage led by a small bent figure in grey.

They emerged within minutes into a cobbled courtyard at the rear of the Abbey, as a dull cloud-filled sky and swirling breeze greeted them. Many voices in the distance could be heard shouting for water, for reinforcements, and as the bells of St Evron cried out across Iola, for God to come to their aid.

The Abbess turned the key in the lock. "Just to be on the safe side," she said with a wry smile.

There were a number of waggons assembled in the courtyard but only one stood ready: two fine silver dappled horses snorted impatiently, already harnessed to one of the larger four-wheeled death waggons. The waggon was wide enough to take two coffins with a narrow bench down each side for mourners or coffin bearers to sit. It bore wooden sides with sliding shutters and curved beams overhead, onto which a toughened leather canopy was held in place with ornate metal studs.

"We have marked the waggon with the sign of the plague," said the Mother Abbess. "Do not take the Slow Road; it will lead you down into the town and within sight of the Abbey. Your best chance is to take the drover's track over the field heading south; circle back around the edge of Iola and head inland, you should pick up the great northern road within the hour." Her eyes lifted to the black smoke curling upwards from the Abbey roof and her lips tightened.

"Go now," said Choi, in earnest. "We are forever in your debt. Go now, and save what you can."

The black smoke was soon accompanied by a display of golden sparks that danced upwards to greet the sky.

"God be with you," she said softly.

"Dear Lord, here you all are," called Father Leon, his sandals flapping against the cobbles as he careered into view having raced along the clifftop: his habit lifted high above his ankles as he ran. "You have little time; Volger has escaped the blaze and is at the front of the Abbey gathering men on horseback to hunt you down." He stopped abruptly, bending forward with hands on knees as he gasped for breath.

"Oh Lordies, Mother Abbess!" he called out. "You must come with me. I beg you. Come with me now," he pleaded. "You must not be seen aiding the Northlanders."

Before she could even open her mouth to protest, he had linked his arm through hers and was steering her back the way he had come: across the cobbles, over the grassy embankment and towards the clifftop walkway. As the two figures in grey rounded the side of the Abbey they beheld the devastation on the seaward side, as the wind gusting inland over the choppy waters fuelled the hungry flames. The Abbess gasped, her eyes widening in horror, as her beloved Abbey surrendered to a horde of flaming tongues.

* * * * * *

Matty flicked the reins with some force; the greys snorted noisily and the waggon lurched forward. Inside, Morven located fresh bread and cheese stored beneath the benches in small hessian sacks, alongside two flagons of ale. As she coaxed Sorcha to drink, the sores around her mouth cracked and bled anew. Nunca frowned and reaching into the pouch at his waist produced a scrap of twisted leather. He pushed a finger inside and scooped out a piece of translucent fat which he gestured to Sorcha he wished to place upon her lips. She shrank back a little, her eyes wary but not hostile, as he smeared the grease upon the infected skin.

Choi, sitting beside Matty upfront, reached beneath the seat and located two monk's habits. "She thought of everything," said Choi, pulling the coarsely woven garment over his head and securing the frayed rope around his waist. He took the reins, as Matty, wriggling about in his seat, struggled into his new outfit.

"I suppose this makes us brothers-in-arms," said Matty, glancing towards Choi with a sly grin. Choi raised an eyebrow as he handed back the reins.

"I suppose it does," he replied.

* * * * * *

"The Slow Road or the steps?" said Jesyka, turning to Aran and Zabian, as they crouched beside the Abbey wall. Without warning, a cohort of mounted soldiers thundered around the side of the Abbey. The Northlanders immediately raised their hoods but did not move. The horses swept past, just an arm's length away, as they raced towards the cobbled courtyard and the Slow Road ahead.

"The steps it is then," said Jesyka, as the last rider disappeared from view.

As they raced towards the top of the steps, Aran found it impossible not to stop and steal a glance back towards the Abbey; where monstrous arms of fire waved frantically from elegant arch-shaped wounds. He felt a tug upon his sleeve.

"We cannot tarry," said Jesyka in earnest. "We must draw the horsemen away. Give them something to chase so that the others have a chance."

Aran grabbed at her hand and held it fast. His eyes searched hers as she met his stare. "I'm sorry about your father…" She raised her free hand and held it to his lips. "And I for your mother," she offered gently.

"Come," called Zabian peering over the edge as the horsemen came into view beneath them. "We won't get a better chance."

Jesyka raced down the steps keeping close to the edge as she aimed her white winged arrows down onto the heads of the leading soldiers. Twice she managed to find exposed flesh at the curve of the neck, where the helmet did not quite meet the body armour. The effect was instant: the victims throwing up their arms, pitching backwards off their mounts, and being instantly trampled by those behind.

"It's the girl!" screamed one of the riders, staring up with wild eyes, before an arrow entered his throat.

Zabian pushed his way through the throng of people at the centre of the steps, most of them racing up towards the Abbey to see the burning spectacle for themselves.

"Perhaps this is God's vengeance," someone called, as they rushed past him. "Or the Devil's," offered another.

Zabian, keeping Jesyka in his sights, focussed on disabling any of Volger's men visible within the crowd. He produced two stubbies from the lining of his coat. They were foot long pieces of smooth rounded wood, which were held at the centre, and had bulbous ends covered in a thin plate of beaten metal. These weapons would allow him to pass undetected through the throng: no blood, no cries.

With searching eyes flickering across the crowd he picked out Volger's unsuspecting men one by one. Moving in close he delivered a sharp upward jab to the diaphragm with one stubby, causing the shocked red-faced recipient to pitch forward; swiftly followed by a downward blow to the back of the head with the other. As they fell unconscious to the floor, Zabian's attention was already on his next victim.

Aran, following at his heel, stooped, and feigning assistance to the prostrate figure, dragged it from beneath the hurrying feet to the right-hand side of the steps. With a quick glance, to ensure no one appeared too interested in his actions, he dug the toe of his boot beneath the man's ribs and flicked him over the edge into the sodden, foul-smelling ditch.

Zabian moved swiftly, and Aran, endeavouring to keep up with his handiwork, found that his breathing became laboured and sweat beaded his body. With only twenty steps to go, he stopped to catch his breath, and watched as the remaining horsemen rounded the corner and gathered at the foot of the steps. At the clatter of horses' hooves upon the cobbles and the menacing shouts of Volger's men, those Eastlanders present upon the lower steps scrambled off the edge into the ditch, leapt the ditch and raced across the grassy hillside, or merely dropped face down, pressing anxious fingers and racing hearts against the cold stone.

Aran could see archers scrambling over the rooftops of the houses opposite, as Jesyka, now with a blade in each hand, crouched on the very edge of the steps. Zabian stood a few paces behind her in the centre, his arms hanging loose by his sides, as he swung the stubbies backwards and forwards to an easy beat. Aran, further back still and to the far right, with a stunned soldier still at his feet, heard steps approaching from behind; as an uncanny stillness heralded Kamron's arrival.

Neither Jesyka nor Zabian turned to acknowledge his presence; but Aran, looking to his left, found him staring straight at him. The left side of his face was covered in copious padding and Aran could clearly see splinters of wood still embedded in the side of his nose, as the one open eye, bloodshot and watering, flickered demonically as he spoke.

"My father has agreed," he said; a definite tremor in his voice, "that all your lives will be spared," he paused, "if Jesyka will remain here as our guest."

Aran could not stop the indignant laughter which escaped him. "And why would your father's word hold any sway with us? We have seen how you accommodate your guests."

"Perhaps," Kamron sneered, "because the only other option is that you *all* die."

The hefty man at Aran's feet suddenly rolled onto his back, opened his eyes and looked up. Aran felt a ring of steel encircle his ankle as the man grabbed him in a vice-like grip and squeezed. As Aran attempted to kick himself free he stumbled towards Kamron. One apprehensive archer, watching from the rooftop, immediately fired an arrow. It pierced Aran's side and threw him back against the steps.

"Hold your fire, you fool," screamed Kamron, with an exaggerated twist of his head, as he sought out the archer with his one seeing eye.

But it was too late. Jesyka, following the arrow's flight, her eyes narrowing as she witnessed it hit its mark, cried out. "Save him Zabian, I beg you. Save his life if you can." And with that she stepped off the edge and dropped effortlessly into the saddle of one of three riderless horses that loitered below.

"Damn it," Kamron cursed, rushing to peer over the edge, just in time to see Jesyka race away through the streets of Iola. He swung round to address the horsemen. "Alive! I tell you. You must take her alive."

He swayed, a little unsteady on his feet, as he stood cradling his head in his hands. Pain flickered across his face, as the watering eye quivered and overflowed.

* * * * * *

As the horsemen sped away, people rose hastily to their feet. Zabian, his face set like stone, swung back his right arm and released the stubby, which spun through the air in a mighty arc until it caught the archer full in the face. Swinging round to face up the steps, he crouched low, and creeping forward lost himself amongst the fast flowing crowd as he made his way to Aran's side. The hefty man was now on his feet and hovered menacingly over him, as Zabian, leaping forward, drove his elbow hard into the side of the man's face.

"Zabian," Aran gasped. "Where is she?"

"She has gone to lead them a merry dance and we must go. Now," he said in earnest, pulling Aran towards him by the shoulders.

Aran stifled a cry as the pain seared through him. "We cannot leave her," he said, his eyes brimming with tears, as he feebly attempted to free himself from Zabian's grip.

"She probably has a better chance of survival than we do," said Zabian sharply. "And this is no time for a debate."

Glancing anxiously across the steps, Zabian could see Kamron pushing through the crowd, his one eye focussed upon the spot where Aran had fallen. Gritting his teeth Zabian swung the second stubby, delivering a swift blow to the side of Aran's head. Aran's face registered a momentary glower of incredulity as his eyelids shuttered to a close.

When Kamron eventually reached the blood stained stone, he bent to retrieve the stubby which gently rocked to and fro upon the edge of the step. Just yards away, with Aran draped across his back, Zabian, cursing under his breath, clambered downhill towards the jetty through the stagnant water-logged ditch.

"Where is Nunca when you need him?" he complained.

* * * * * *

Sparks flew from the horse's iron shoes as it hurtled headlong through the cobbled streets of Iola. Crossing the wooden swing bridge that straddled the muddy estuary, Jesyka entered the northern side of the town; looking back she counted seven riders in pursuit fast approaching the bridge. The road along the northerly quayside lay eerily quiet; many inhabitants having already crossed the estuary in order to aid those fighting the fire, or merely feast upon the clifftop spectacle.

Racing on past the many ships at anchor, Jesyka found herself with only one option: a steep slipway that led directly onto the vast sandy shoreline.

"Nothing else for it," she said, as she patted the horse's neck, dug her knees into its ribs, and drove the beast headlong down onto the fine-grained sand.

She was thankful for the sharp colder air which flew at her face, cooling her skin and tossing her hair. On hitting the sand, however, Jesyka realised that the horses would find this terrain more demanding: rapidly tiring their muscles and draining their strength.

Rolling waves broke repeatedly upon the shore, spilling out across the yielding sand, before summoned back by the pull of a playful moon. And the wind, urging the breakers forward, whistled along in perfect harmony with the thundering roar of a lively sea. Stretching further than the eye could see the golden shore appeared almost colourless in the drab light of a waning day.

Jesyka laid her head against the animal's damp muscular neck as its breathing became shallower and its speed lessened. With heightening waves to the right, rocky embankment to the left, and miles of endless sand ahead, Jesyka glanced back to see that her pursuers, beating their mounts incessantly, were gaining upon her. "Well done, old girl," she whispered. "This is where we part company."

Jesyka reined in her mount, who snorted with relief, steam soaring from its sweating coat. She leapt from its back and began to clamber up the steep boulder-strewn banking which led to the headland.

"There's no way out for her," called the lead rider to his men.

"I wouldn't be too sure about that," cried another, as he watched open-mouthed at Jesyka's rapid ascent, as she leapt rock to rock with unnatural speed. "Dear Lord, look at her go."

"Don't just watch, you idiot, get after her," he roared. "And you," he bellowed to the last horseman who had just arrived on the scene, "you're handy with a bow, I'll see you get an extra month's pay if you can take her down before she reaches the top. But remember," he smirked, "they want her alive."

As she charged heavenward, pumping arms propelling her forward, eyes fixed upon the summit now only feet away, the arrow struck. She heard the jubilant whooping from the men on the beach as the archer found his mark. The arrow entered the back of her thigh and drove deep. She whelped with shock as much as agony, as she dragged her damaged leg up and over the edge.

"Remount," ordered the lead rider, a grin flashing across his face. "She'll not get far now. Head back to the town, then up onto the headland," he glanced towards the horizon, as darker clouds rolled in off the sea. "We'll have her before this day is done."

23

Captain Quiggs placed the ever handy bottle of dark sticky rum on the table before him and placed two small glasses down beside it. He watched as Zabian lowered himself into the chair opposite.

"I take it the young buck will not be joining us?" said Captain Quiggs, as he raised an eyebrow.

"Your assumption is correct, my friend. He will struggle to stomach food for a day or two, let alone strong drink." Zabian released his cloak and stretched out his long aching limbs. "He will no doubt curse and cry himself to exhaustion."

"Well, he's making a good job of it. I'll venture he never bawled so heartily since the day he entered the world, and some old nurse held him by the ankles and slapped his rosy cheeks," offered the Captain, as he poured with a steady hand and filled both glasses.

The merest glimmer of a smile played upon Zabian's lips as he reached forward to embrace the proffered drink.

"The physical wound will heal well enough. He is young. But the inner wounds are raw and deep." Zabian poured the contents of the glass down his throat in one swift action and returned it to the table. "Until he has had the luxury of a little time in which to embrace his pain, and accept what he has seen, and what he now knows – he will suffer a good while yet."

"A woman?" enquired the Captain, settling himself into his old leather-bound chair, which creaked in protest; his eyes never leaving Zabian's troubled face.

"Women," said Zabian, as Captain Quiggs leant forward and refilled the empty glasses, "would be more accurate. A mother he thought was dead is alive: having spent four years in a living hell. And now he has lost Jesyka – for a while at least."

"Women and pain – an inescapable combination," offered the Captain, raising his glass.

Zabian's eyes finally met those of the Captain, as they simultaneously emptied a second glass.

"I would surmise that you have some experience in this field?" ventured the Captain.

A furtive smile spread across Zabian's face as he laid his empty glass down with some force. "You are a wily old fox, Captain Quiggs, and no mistake. Your intuition does you credit." He stared at the glass. "I have loved but one woman in my life taken from me by a circumstance of birth and a scheming brother."

Captain Quiggs' eyes widened with an expectant look upon his face as he hastily replenished Zabian's glass.

"But your wealth is immense," said the Captain. "Such wealth as you possess is this no comfort?"

Zabian rotated the refilled glass between his fingers. "Sadly no, my friend; but I will admit it has its uses." His smile grew broader. "One day, Captain, when I am not so weary, I will tell you my story." He slid slowly down in his seat and raised his bejewelled boots to rest upon the table.

Captain Quiggs, reaching forward, retrieved the full glass still set before Zabian and watched, now with a glass in each hand, as his companion's eyes closed and he slipped away into an exhausted sleep.

"I look forward to that encounter, Mr Zabian," whispered the Captain, as he tapped the glasses together and promptly drained them both.

24

With trembling fingers Jesyka rubbed at the moisture that repeatedly sprang to life upon her forehead; her face almost unrecognisable as it contorted with pain. She clenched her teeth and levered herself upright. As she lowered her left foot gingerly to the ground, she turned to face the shore, drawing in sharp salty gusts of air that blasted in from the sea.

"I must run, run like the wind," she gasped.

Though the light was dim she could clearly make out flat open fields all around. There was nowhere to go to ground; nowhere to hide. She had to run. As she moved off her screams were carried on the wind as she fought to find a rhythm and pace that she could sustain; and yet all the while knowing that she was moving too slowly, far too slowly. As her shallow breathing settled she focussed only on blocking the pain, drawing on every fibre in her body and every beat of her heart to suppress the fire that raged in her thigh.

Though it felt like an eternity, Jesyka had no sense of how long she had been on the move, when she felt the distinct thud of horses' hooves pounding the earth. Directly ahead she spotted the dark silhouette of a small copse of trees rising up from the middle of a field.

"So, father, is it all to end here, like this?" An anxious laugh burst from her. "Perhaps I shall be with you sooner than either of us thought."

On reaching the copse Jesyka threw herself to the ground and began to crawl amongst the fallen leaves and dense dry bracken. She could feel herself in danger of drifting away into unconsciousness, as the pain from her thigh throbbed upwards through her heart and into her head. She battled with the nausea and the distorted vision, knowing that only by remaining conscious could she remain invisible.

Her head suddenly burst into life, teeming with brilliantly coloured images: Methna preparing food; Choi smoking his pipe; Rion baying on the hillside; Jaclan running, running for his life with the horsemen after him; Raghnall dying and Aran...

"Father, give me strength," she cried out. "Keep me strong. Do not let me fall..."

And as she lay upon the earth she could feel the dull beat of horses drawing ever closer; she heard them snorting, blowing out hot foul smelling air, and as she drifted away she felt certain she could hear the howling of wolves.

* * * * * *

"There she is," cried the lead rider, "there, at the foot of the oak."

As the seven breathless riders gathered together, they formed a line and cautiously began to move forward. "Now, we've got the slippery little vixen," he yelled, his eyes aglow with excitement. "But don't take any chances. You've seen what she's capable of. I, for one, will not be happy till we've got her trussed up like a goose ready for the pot."

"Hey, listen, do you hear that?" said one of the others, standing tall in his stirrups and looking down from the copse across the open land to the west.

"Stay focussed you idiot. Don't take your eyes off her

– she may make a run for it," hissed the lead rider, as with a coil of rope in hand he made ready to dismount.

"Yeah, I can hear it," called another. "That's wolves that is, and no mistake; strange time of day for them to be making such a racket."

"Lord almighty, here they come," cried a third. "There's at least a dozen, if not more, and they're heading this way."

With Akir and Kyler out in front, the pack leapt out from the edge of Estril Forest and bounded across the open ground snarling and snapping at the air as they flew across the field heading for the trees.

The horses sensing imminent danger reared up in unison, as with startled eyes and frantic neighs they attempted to flee.

"Hold them steady," screamed the lead rider, "we must bag the girl. We can deal with this lot. Hold your nerve, you block-heads."

As the pack bounded headlong up the hill and burst through the trees, the horses began screeching and frantically kicking out as anxiety transformed into sheer terror. The riders, struggling to hold their mounts, watched in amazement as the pack spread out in front of them; forming a formidable barrier and denying them access to Jesyka's body. Akir thrust her snout into Jesyka's neck, and satisfying herself that she was alive, threw back her head and pierced the air with a bloodcurdling howl.

"They've come for the girl!" called out one of the soldiers. "This is nothing short of the Devil's work."

"Shut up you idiot!" screamed the lead rider.

Having located their prize, Akir and Kyler turned to face the enemy. With menacing growls forming deep within their throats, and saliva dripping from their soft jowls, they barred their fangs. The rest of the pack joined with them as they began to advance.

"Kill the lead pair. Do it – do it now!" called out the lead rider, perspiration streaming down his face.

As the soldiers fought to control the terror-stricken beasts beneath them, the pack continued to push steadily forward, as with heads held low they snapped repeatedly in the direction of the horses' legs.

"These are no ordinary wolves. You kill them if you dare. I'm out of here," cried out one of the soldiers, as he loosened his reins and let the horse bolt headlong out of the trees and back towards Iola.

"Hold your ground, I say hold your ground!" the lead rider screamed, as his flushed face convulsed with anger. His terrified horse, rearing up violently, threw him to the ground. Scrambling to his feet he cursed and swore, as he watched his mount tear away down the hillside, followed by the remaining horses with their riders intact.

"Volger will hear of this cowardice," he screeched after them.

He remained with his back to the pack, as his breathing grew ever shallower and the florid face paled and twisted. With trembling fingers he finally managed to fix an arrow into his bow. Hesitating just for a moment, he spun round, dropped to one knee, and aimed straight into the pack. The instantaneous cry told him he had hit flesh and a faint smile began to play upon his lips but not for long.

* * * * * *

Balac was only three miles from home when without warning Akir and Kyler leapt out from the side of the road directly in front of Olran.

"What in heaven's name are you doing here," Balac shouted, "you'll be skinned and in the pot before sun-up showing yourselves in these parts."

Akir and Kyler having left the others keeping watch over Jesyka, had headed out in search of Balac. He dropped down from his horse and stroked their heads. Their coats were hot as their bodies heaved from the exertion and long dry tongues hung from the side of their mouths. Akir's legs trembled and she lay down just for a moment, staggering back onto her feet almost immediately; her bloodshot eyes telling Balac that they had run many miles in search of him.

Sensing the urgency, Balac remounted. "Alright, alright, let's go," he called. Olran, laden down with provisions, snorted her displeasure, as they left the road and headed out across the countryside at a fearsome pace.

* * * * * *

On reaching the copse Balac jumped down from Olran's back and ran through the pack, dropping to his knees beside the two she-wolves who lay by Jesyka's side. He had seen the carcass of one wolf with an arrow in its neck and could hardly imagine what had occurred in this place. He grabbed a handful of amber hair and raised Jesyka's head from the ground.

Akir shouldered her way to the front of the pack and whimpered over Jesyka, licking her face and pushing her head from side to side with her snout. Balac spotted the broken arrow still embedded in Jesyka's thigh and frowned. "Akir," he said, pushing her aside, "away with you, I must get her back to the house."

As her cloak fell open, he was startled to see the breastplate and the weaponry. "Who are you," he asked in wonder, "that the wolves would lay down their lives for you?"

He slipped his hand beneath the breastplate and pressed hard against her heart. It beat still, but far too fast, as her lips parted and a gentle sigh escaped. The wolves instantly began to howl in unison as Balac, struck by the strangeness of their mood, gathered Jesyka into his arms and manoeuvred her up onto Olran's back. As he held her upright before him, his hand clamped over her racing heart, he monitored the beat, whispering words of comfort that she was safe and he would heal her.

Part Three:
Reckoning

25

Aran's wound was mending fast; in no small part due to the skill of the *Dancing Monkey's* resident healer. The healer's androgynous appearance prompted many bemused glances and much spirited speculation. His limbs, long and overly slender, seemed at odds with his large round eyes and fine facial features. His skin shone, resembling highly polished mahogany, and his black wispy shoulder-length hair was held back from his face by a multi-coloured beaded band.

The healer's quiet incessant chanting, as he tended Aran's wound, appeared to entrance the young man into a state of utter tranquillity. Zabian found himself reaching for the door, sensing that he too was being drawn under some captivating spell merely by being in the vicinity of such strange incantations.

Captain Quiggs simply shrugged when Zabian queried the man's origin and the nature of his medicine. "He eats little, takes up little space, and is the finest ship's healer I ever came across. Though I don't dispute he's something strange to look upon, and his methods are," he added, with a grimace, "somewhat unusual."

* * * * * *

After three days at sea, Aran was woken by Captain Quiggs bellowing the order to trim the sails, as the *Dancing Monkey* became ensnarled in an unexpected troublesome squall. The vessel suddenly bucked and rolled violently, her timbers groaning with annoyance at the heightening swell. He listened for some minutes to the pounding of feet overhead and the raised voices of the crew, as they responded readily to their Captain's commands.

The door to Aran's tiny cabin swung open, and Zabian, bending low, stepped inside. He reached the bed in one step and attempted, somewhat awkwardly in so confined a space, to settle himself on the end of the narrow cot.

"The healer appears pleased with your progress, judging by the amount of nodding and grinning he does," said Zabian. "But for the life of me I cannot make sense of a single word he utters."

"I have no complaints," said Aran, smiling weakly.

As the sailors continued to race to and fro, their hammering feet booming like thunder overhead, Zabian took a deep breath and exhaled slowly.

"Aran, I know that you feel a great weight upon your mind and in your heart for there is much for you to be concerned about." He paused. "But whatever lies ahead, I would have you know this, Lord of the Northland – we will stay by your side until this battle with Volger is done."

"And can you speak so freely for your friends?" Aran asked, forcing back the lump that rose in his throat.

"Indeed," exclaimed Zabian, with a wry smile. "For what else would they do with their time?"

"And Jesyka?"

"She drew them away, in an attempt to save your life," he stated, the muscles softening in his face, as the smile grew into a grin. "And she succeeded. She usually does."

Aran felt his eyes begin to sting.

"Besides," Zabian continued, "I am a betting man and I would put my money on Jesyka every time." He rose to his feet and stepped towards the door. As he reached for the handle he hesitated. "Have hope, my young friend, and cling to it."

Aran closed his eyes; finally allowing the gnawing agony of not knowing where she was, or what had happened to her, to course unfettered through his veins. When this dull, unrelenting pain eventually came to rest deep within his soul, it was a pain unlike any he had ever known.

* * * * * *

On the seventh day after leaving Iola, Zabian and Aran stepped ashore to be greeted by the first flakes of winter snow. One became two, two became three, and then, as the sky grew milky white, the heavens opened, and a multitude of giant flakes fluttered down to cool the earth and ease its pain.

Aran was conscious that he saw nothing now through those naive young eyes that had headed south filled with energy, hope and wonder. As they walked on through the whitening land, he grimaced at the twinge in his side and felt his heart heavy within. He had thought much about what he might say to his father, as he lay staring up at the lantern in his cabin which swung like the pendulum of a clock: marking the seconds, the minutes and the hours as they passed; but he had failed to reach beyond the rage which engulfed him at the image of his mother prostrate within that hideous cage.

When they finally entered Kinfallon Castle, he headed straight for the central staircase; his anger, which had been mounting since he first sighted the castle in the distance, propelled him towards his father's chamber. When he burst through the door he found his father in conversation with Methna.

"My son!" Broehain exclaimed joyfully. "Dear Lord be praised you are back – and your sister?"

"And Jesyka?" asked Methna nervously, her eyes searching expectantly.

Tears rolled easily now from Aran's hollow eyes as he crossed the room and stood before his father: close enough to feel his father's breath upon his face. "Your deception, father, your weakness has cost us all so dear," he said, forcing the words into his father's face. Broehain's legs faltered and he clutched at Methna for support.

"Morven?" he gasped, his shoulders heaving as he struggled for breath.

"She lives, yes, yes, she lives," Aran cried, as unnatural laughter accompanied his tears. "As does my mother!" he roared, clutching at his father's shoulders as if he were attempting to push him down into some abyss.

"Lord be praised," gasped Broehain, struggling to remain standing under the pressure of his son's grip.

"How can this be? What does this mean?" asked Methna in alarm. "Aran please – where are the others?"

Zabian appeared in the doorway. "Aran, let your father be, this is not the time or the place," he commanded. "Leave him now. You must look to yourself; your wound must not be inflamed."

He moved further into the room. "Aran, as Lord of the Northland – I beseech you to think of your people. We have much to attend to and so little time, and you have a nation to lead."

Aran, releasing his father, swung round to face him. "What is this nonsense that you speak? I, lead the Northland?"

"What say you, King Broehain, is it not now your wish that your son should rule in your place?" Zabian's unsmiling face beheld Broehain's bewildered vacant stare. "Sorcha, where is my Sorcha?" he murmured, slipping away from Methna's support.

"Aran, he is a broken man. The explanations can wait," said Zabian.

Aran's head pounded and invisible hands seemed to twist and squeeze at his very core, as he backed away from his father.

"It is good to see you Zabian," said Methna weakly, searching his face with troubled eyes. "You look as though you could also do with a little attention."

As Zabian turned to meet her gaze she shivered, as if a sudden chill had passed through her. He stood, with stooped shoulders, as though a mighty weight bore down upon him, and an overwhelming sense of sadness hung in the air.

"We must walk a while together Methna," he said in a gentle voice, as he held out his hand towards her.

26

On their return to Iola, the terror-stricken horsemen were immediately summoned to appear before Kamron. They continually interrupted one another as they told and retold their fantastical tale; which grew to epic proportions in their desperate efforts to justify their failure to capture the girl.

On his initial visit to the site, Kamron saw for himself the carcass of the wolf with the arrow through its neck and the disfigured remains of the lead rider. Much to his men's amusement, Kamron continued to revisit the copse; for although he had had to concede that their story held at least a modicum of truth, the mystery remained as to what had happened to Jesyka.

Behind raised hands, they would snigger about how he would crouch beneath the oak with a wistful expression upon his face. Kamron insisted they were there to look for clues, potentially missed during earlier searches; but these men had their own theory, having witnessed how earnestly he had pleaded with Volger to spare her life. Never before had they observed the son take on the might of his father with so much vigour. Kamron argued forcibly that controlling the heir, rather than merely disposing of her, would offer more options in their final push to take the Northland.

Volger, being initially infuriated by this suggestion, came to recognise that the notion was not totally without merit.

His rages, however, at the loss of all his prisoners, and especially the inconclusive whereabouts of Jesyka, continued to resurface. After one incident, during dinner, where he had suddenly begun to beat the table with his fists, until they were bruised and bloodied, Kamron sought to deflect his father's attention to other matters.

With the knowledge that heavy snow would soon deny them access to the north of the Eastland and all of the Northland, Kamron suggested that they revisit their conquests in the west and south; essentially to ensure that those entrusted with stabilising these territories were fulfilling their commissions with sufficient rigour.

All soldiers conscripted from within the occupied nations of the Great Crossland were allowed to journey home for the duration of the winter. Their pledges to return, ready and willing to fight for their Supreme Leader, when commanded to do so, were guaranteed by the threat of retribution against their families if they did not. Volger had enhanced the process by ensuring that each man witnessed his name being entered into a ledger, and so strengthening the notion that the promise of reprisal was no empty threat, but as certain as night following day.

Many of Volger's longer-serving soldiers, who had travelled with him from overseas, were to remain and work in Iola under the command of the master craftsmen, who gathered to begin the long arduous business of restoration. Many of these artisans so beloved their craft that they would labour daily from the first light of dawn until the sun slid from the sky. There was work enough here to last a man's lifetime and beyond; for one half of the great Abbey now lay mangled at their feet: a form-less pile of blackened and shattered stone that spewed its debris out towards the cliff edge.

* * * * * *

The damage to Kamron's sight in his left eye proved permanent; splinters of wood, having been painstakingly extracted one by one, had resulted in a plethora of tell-tale scars that speckled the side of his face. When he smiled, which was seldom, sharp pin-pricks of pain ricocheted through the dappled skin: a constant reminder that many more minute slivers of wood lay embedded beneath the surface. From time to time a rogue splinter would tunnel its way towards freedom, causing pus to gather at the site, and requiring the resultant angry skin to be lanced: adding yet another blemish to the already flawed profile.

27

Balac rearranged the interior of his cabin to accommodate his unexpected guest. He gave up his bed to Jesyka and constructed himself a simple hessian hammock lined with an array of animal skins.

He realised that the removal of the arrow was crucial to her chances of survival but did not relish the task. During his years spent wandering the desert lands, and witnessing the aftermath of violent skirmishes between feuding tribesmen, he had acquired some knowledge regarding the treatment of various wounds. He was, however, only to well aware that this had been gained by mere observation.

The shaft of the arrow appeared loose within the wound and a slight twist caused it to rotate easily. Balac frowned. This potentially meant that the arrowhead had more than likely become detached. Peering closely at the front of her thigh he could see a slight discoloured bulge and the unmistakable metal tip sitting just beneath the surface. Balac repositioned his grip around the shaft and tentatively began to pull: drawing it out from its point of entry. He exhaled loudly, thankful that the procedure had proved quick and simple. The removal of the arrowhead, however, was a much more daunting prospect.

Jesyka never fully regained consciousness during those first few days, though her breathing settled into a regular, gentler rhythm and she readily took sips of water when a spoon was pressed against her lips. As the circle of raised skin reddened and swelled, Balac knew that he could delay no longer.

He sharpened his finest hunting knife, dousing the blade in boiling water. As he watched her fitfully slip in and out of sleep, he realised that what was troubling him most was the possibility that she might move during the procedure. Having decided that he could not take the risk, he bound her to the bed using the reins from Olran's bridle: securing her across the shoulders, the hips and above the knees. He shooed Akir and Kyler outside; their penetrating, ever-watchful eyes and pitiful whimpering proving an unwelcome distraction.

Balac knelt, knife in hand. He hesitated, looked around the cabin and then up towards the ceiling. "Whoever is watching over you, I hope they're paying attention."

To his delight, as he lanced the skin, the offending tip almost ejected itself, appearing to be projected forward by the foul matter that had gathered around it. Balac sat back upon his heels; relief etched upon his face as he glanced heavenward and grinned.

* * * * * *

Jesyka drew her first conscious breath of air in almost a week, and raising herself up onto her elbows glanced around the cabin. Her surroundings felt strangely familiar; the odd looking hammock drawing a smile to her face. The space was clean and sparsely furnished with a store of firewood neatly stacked in one corner. Lifting the blanket she stared down at the heavy binding around her thigh and scowled.

She sat on the edge of the bed and pressed the soles of her feet to the timber floor. It felt good even to experience this simple sensation as the cooler air swirled around her ankles and the hairs on her skin lifted. Rising gingerly to her feet, Jesyka hobbled towards the door. She was instantly aware of her weakened state, as she struggled with the stiff, ill-fitting bolts; a low deep-throated grunt accompanying her effort to swing the door open. A frail winter sun instantly bathed her from head to toe in soft golden light. She closed her eyes, tilted her face to catch every gentle ray, and basked in its warm and tender caress.

It was dusk when Balac entered the cottage that day, flecks of snow glistening in his hair, and beheld, much to his surprise, a roaring fire and Jesyka, with freshly washed and tidied hair sitting by the hearth.

"So, it is you I have to thank," she said, fixing him with steady eyes.

"And a bunch of demonic wolves," he replied, as Akir and Kyler pushed past him.

28

Matty jumped down from the waggon, his face aglow as he stared ahead at the faint outline of the castle. "I cannot believe we actually made it," he said.

"We were lucky," offered Choi.

Morven moved forward and slipped her hand into Matty's as she lifted moist eyes to gaze upon her home.

"How is she?" he asked, gently squeezing her hand.

"It is incredible how much she has improved, her skin heals, her hair grows – but her mind…" she turned her face to meet his, a slight tremor catching at her bottom lip, "I can hardly think what to say to my father."

"This is as far as the waggon will go," called Choi. "We must abandon it here and proceed on foot. The snow is too deep."

Nunca, wrapping Sorcha tightly within his blanket, stepped from the tailgate of the waggon.

"If you disappear in the snow, little friend," he said, throwing Choi a wry smile. "I'll come back and carry you too."

Choi ignored him; but as soon as Nunca turned his back and began to pound the snow into submission, Choi furtively followed in his tracks. Sorcha smiled, seemingly enjoying the snow's gentle touch upon her face; as Nunca, with head bent and eyes half closed, focussed upon the looming walls of Kinfallon Castle and the home Queen Sorcha had not entered for more than four years.

* * * * * *

Torpen and Zabian stood together, looking out from Torpen's chamber, when the death waggon slowly emerged from the gusting snow swirls that filled the chasm between earth and sky. The waggon stopped. Zabian held his breath, counting the occupants as they alighted.

"All present and correct," he stated with a thankful sigh. "The youngsters have shown great courage."

"Indeed," Torpen smiled, "though I doubt they would have survived their ordeal without your direction."

The great castle doors creaked open far beneath them, and Zabian, bending forward to peer down, heard King Broehain's cry shatter the still whiteness as he ran forward. He stumbled almost immediately into the great drifts that encased the castle walls, as two young attendants lunged after him, catching at his robes and lifting him upright. Zabian frowned.

"That may be so. But now they understand, only too well, the true nature of the threat that faces them. They have learnt quickly and well."

"And Jesyka?"

"Will come, if she can," said Zabian, the muscles tightening in his face. "I would stake my life upon it."

* * * * * *

When Zabian had broken the news to Methna about Raghnall and Jesyka, she had left the confines of the castle and headed back to her cottage in Felden Forest. Three weeks on, and with the safe arrival of the others, Aran headed out in the hope of persuading her to return to Kinfallon, before the great freeze squeezed the final vestiges of life from the already torpid land.

As Aran stepped over the threshold, his heart surged as he struggled to suppress images from that earlier time when they had gathered here. He remembered his impatience, the excitement, the uncertainty… He stood before a dying fire and realised that Methna was watching him from the shadows. Turning to face her, he blushed slightly, realising that she had been studying his altered profile: three two-inch scars that stood proud upon his right cheek.

"Our lives are much altered since we first met," she said quietly. "Some of our scars are visible," she paused, "and some are not."

As he glanced around the still, now bare room, he noted with some surprise that two packed bags already sat upon the copper-topped table and that Methna wore a full-length outdoor coat of red fox fur.

"I see you have pre-empted my visit," he smiled weakly, "and presumably also my request that you return to the castle. For now it is time to plan our defence." Aran stared back at the fire. "Perhaps there may be some comfort in working and waiting together…"

Methna approached the fire and kicked cold grey ash over the remaining glowing embers. She turned to Aran and looking up into his downcast face, grasped his hands within her own.

"She will come," she said.

Aran attempted to calm his constricting throat.

"She will come," she repeated. "I came out here to grieve for my husband, as you know, and also to pray for Jesyka. I came to lay my heart quiet; not to deny my pain or to force it away, but merely to listen to all it could tell me." She paused and Aran felt her small fine fingers press deeper into his palms.

"Rion came and stood in the clearing before my door, he pawed at the earth until I opened it and as I stepped out I felt a keen wind blowing from the Eastland, and upon it from afar came the sound of howling wolves. As I reached out to touch his mighty head more than a hundred deer appeared from the forest behind him; for they had all heard that cry upon the wind."

Methna released his hands. "She lives. That is what they came to tell me." Her voice broke a little, but her eyes were smiling. "And if she lives, she will come."

She backed away and approaching an old battered chest that sat by the door, lifted the lid which creaked in protest. She raised an object wrapped in blue linen and shook the content free. Aran beheld a breastplate of toughened hide; the head of a bear, its teeth bared, was riveted to the front and fashioned in the smoothest silver that he had ever seen.

"The white bear, from the far north?" he asked; a stupefied expression upon his face.

"Indeed," she replied. "Do you know of the Weyland people?" she asked, her cheeks glowing.

"I have heard tales, but have seen only one. One who came to trade skins when I was very small."

"They are my people, the Weylanders of the white plains and the white skies." Her fingers traced the outline of the silver face. "And the white bear."

Bending forward for a second time, Methna reached deeper into the chest and dragged out a heavier bundle wrapped tightly in coarse hessian and tied with black string. Laying the package on top of the chest she slit the brittle binding, releasing a pelt of dense white fur that unfurled to reveal a stash of six fighting blades of various lengths. The weapons were thickly smeared in a yellowy grey grease, and as the smell of rancid fat rose into the air, Aran jerked his head away.

"Disgusting," said Methna, wrinkling her nose. "Let's hope it's done the job."

She lifted the largest blade from its cocoon and rubbed vigorously at the hilt. Aran held his breath and bent to watch as the letter M rose from the grime. The letter had been constructed using the image of two intertwined snakes with ferocious gaping jaws and over-long fangs.

"They belong to you?"

"A gift from my father forged by Weyland's master blacksmith, Yorcum. He presented me with these blades when I chose to move south and take Raghnall for my husband." She smiled. "He joked that if the marriage was a disaster, I could always fight my way back home – for no blade forged within the Northland could match their strength or beauty."

"I had thought that by bringing you to the castle, I could have offered you some protection." He shrugged. "Now I see that you, like your daughter, are quite capable of looking after yourself."

"Every weapon will be needed to take on the might of Volger," she said, curling both hands around its hilt, as she lifted it to greet the shaft of sunlight that stole in through the open door. "Every sword, knife, and arrow…" She turned to meet his gaze. "And anyone who can raise a blade from its sheath will be needed to join this fight."

29

"It will take time," said Balac, a heavy frown darkening his face.

"That's the last thing I have," snapped Jesyka. "You know that." She gritted her teeth and pushing down with weakened arms, raised herself to a sitting position. She moaned with the effort; the colour draining from her face.

"You've pushed yourself too hard," he said sullenly.

Jesyka breathed heavily in and out through her nose, attempting to control the nausea that pounded in her ears as the room swayed. Her arms finally gave way, as with a frustrated groan she fell back against the pillow.

Balac backed away from the bed. "Accept it. You're going nowhere fast."

Jesyka's fists thumped the bed, as cursing under her breath she forced her eyes to open again. Balac returned to stand over her with a bowl of steaming soup in his hand. "You are the most badly behaved, ungrateful wretch I have ever encountered."

Though exasperation consumed her, Jesyka could not withhold a feeble snort of laughter that rose to meet the scolding face that tut-tutted overhead.

"And why am I not going anywhere fast?" she gasped.

"Because during the days that you have spent bed-ridden, due to your witless frolics, something has occurred," he said.

Walking towards the door of the cabin, he threw back the bolts and gently drew the door open. Jesyka, raising her still thumping head merely inches from the bed, peered through bloodshot eyes at a wall of glistening snow that sparkled in the light of the fire.

She squeezed her eyes shut but failed to stop the tears of frustration as they trickled down her temples and ran into her hair. He was right, she knew it; she had pushed herself too hard.

It was just over five weeks since he had entered the cottage to find her sitting by the hearth. He had warned her from the outset not to underestimate the severity of the wound: suggesting eight more weeks before she could even consider planning her journey north.

Each day, with the snow as yet only slight upon the ground, Balac had spent the shrinking daylight hours snaring birds and hares: with the necessity now to provide for two. Though Jesyka spent the evenings quiet enough before the fire, during the day she had taken to venturing out of doors, impatient to prove that she might yet beat the worst of the winter weather. Day by day she grew stronger, walking with Akir by her side through the forest and at intervals breaking into a gentle run.

As the weeks passed she began to jump streams, climb trees and routinely track animals to their lairs: merely for the fun of it. At the end of each day Balac would often return to find her bringing in firewood and berate her heartily not to over-exert herself.

Jesyka had decided that the time had come to confess to Balac about her daily excursions, and her opinion that she was more than ready to journey north without delay. She recognised that she owed this man a huge debt of gratitude and felt a sudden pang of sadness to be leaving his company. She had grown used to his ways, living in so confined a space; those evenings of talking and long silences having resulted in an easy playful friendship. Leaving, she realised, would not be as easy as she had envisaged. And then she fell.

Each day she had strived to climb an even taller tree than the day before. Having been raised in the forest, this habitat was like a playground to her; but when the sun, suddenly dipping out of sight, caused an immediate change in the colours and contrasts of the woodland, she misjudged her final descent of the day.

Rotten wood creaked and quivered beneath her feet, as Jesyka, landing on a diseased limb, caused a deep crack to form along its length. With tired muscles slow to react, she failed to maintain her balance and toppled from her treetop perch. Gathering momentum, she collided with lower branches; her right thigh taking a direct hit as she plunged downward.

When Balac returned home he found her trembling before the fire, peeling off her blood-sodden clothes with unsteady fingers.

"Dear God, what has happened?" he asked, dropping his catch upon the floor.

As she lifted a remorseful, ashen face to meet his gaze, she stumbled forward, landing on all fours at his feet. Crying out with frustration and fury at her own recklessness, she surrendered to the arms that raised her effortlessly from the floor.

30

Aran strode towards the Great Hall with Matty by his side.

"Decisions need to be made, Matty. We can wait no longer."

"Do you think the Council has the stomach for this fight?" asked Matty.

"We will see soon enough," said Aran, marching through the open door and making his way towards the assembled crowd.

Morven stepped forward to greet them both, placing a hand upon each.

"The guardians will join us shortly," she said.

Raising her eyes to Aran, she squeezed his arm. "I am with you heart and soul, brother. My loyalty lies with you."

Aran placed his lips softly against her forehead. "This will take some getting used to." He grinned.

Morven reddened and pursed her lips. "That does not mean I will not disagree with you when I think fit," she replied, pulling a face over her shoulder as she turned away.

Stifling a grin, Aran watched her with gentle eyes, as he took his seat at the table.

Torpen, occupying a well-padded chair beside the fire, made no attempt to join them; while Ferneth, deep in slumber, lay curled at his feet.

"Come, Torpen," said Aran, reaching out with a

welcoming arm.

"I must decline," he replied. "I am part of the past, not the future. The heir is found and I can do no more. It is not for me to influence what is to come."

He turned his head and stared into the flames. "But with all my heart I wish you God's wisdom," he muttered.

"And what of the heir? Where is she?" asked Lord Aonghus of Gyllra.

"We will come to that," said Aran. "But first I must speak of my father."

Aran cleared his throat. "King Broehain will take no part in future Council gatherings or decision making." He raised his voice, ignoring the furtive glances. "He remains King of the Northland in name only." He paused. "As many of you already know, he spends much of his time with Queen Sorcha, and this for now is all his fragile health will allow."

Colour rose to his face as he continued. "I have no intention of shirking my duty, and at my father's behest, I come to pledge my life to you – each and every one of you – and to our nation." He looked slowly round the table, acknowledging every pair of eyes that rose to meet his own. "I come before you today to work with you in determining how we choose to meet this imminent threat of war. For be in no doubt, that when winter releases its grip, Volger's fist will beat upon our door and demand the keys of our kingdom."

"If we are to fight, do we have a hope in heaven or hell?" asked Lord Gwawl of Ganus.

"That I cannot answer," said Aran. "We imagine his numbers will prove far greater than our own – but have no way of knowing exactly what size of force he can muster or what weight of weaponry he will bring to bear against us."

"And what are our options if we do not fight? To surrender? To run?" offered Lord Aonghus.

Many of the Lords met these suggestions with scowls of derision and shaking heads; as dark, anxious glances ricocheted around the table.

"Since our return, we have relayed in detail our experiences of 'visiting' the Eastland," replied Aran. "Therefore no one should be in any doubt of what our land would become under his rule."

"But should we consider getting some of our people out?" stated Lord Gwawl flatly. "Though it gives me no pleasure to suggest it."

"Those left to fight would be fewer but would that realistically have any bearing on the outcome?" asked Lord Aonghus.

"It is my intention to stay and fight," said Aran. "But with the likelihood being that the odds will be against us, I would not ask any man or woman who does not wish to commit to this fight to stay." Silence hung heavy in the air before Aran continued. "There will, however, be limited opportunities for people to leave whilst the snow lies so heavy across our land."

"And what of the guardians?" asked Lord Gwawl.

"The guardians have pledged to stand beside us; they offer their skills and themselves to our cause. And Jesyka will return to lead us." He spoke with conviction, willing himself to believe. "However, we must make preparations now as best we can. For we must not squander what little time we have."

Ferneth raised her head and watched with half shut eyes as the door creaked open and Methna, Zabian, Nunca and Choi entered the room. They each raised a hand in greeting to those ensconced at the table; before settling themselves around the hearth beside Torpen and Ferneth.

The discussions continued and the hours passed, with the need for food and drink to be ferried into the chamber.

When the robust voices of the Council grew curiously quiet, Ferneth yawned, shook her head, and rose stiffly to stand upon unsteady legs.

Aran drew a deep breath and rose to his feet; arching out his aching back and pressing his chest forward. "Then we are in agreement," he said, glancing towards the guardians who rose collectively to their feet and came to stand around the table.

"Firstly, here at Kinfallon and in every district the black-smith's forge will never sleep – metal will be commandeered for the production of arms – so that each day we will see their numbers rise. This Great Hall will become the main armoury; being in the inner sanctum of the castle it should be the last to fall if we are breached.

"Secondly, we will accept anyone who chooses to stay and fight. Those who volunteer, who are not trained fighting men or women, will receive immediate instruction.

"And thirdly, we will attempt to evacuate a number of complete families from each region via sledges along frozen rivers to the coast – where we will muster a fleet of ships to sail north towards Weyland. The first ship to sail will have the Snake Sword of Methna onboard to be presented to the Weylanders with a request for shelter and protection for their cousins from the south." He sighed. "Then, at least should the worst happen – there is a chance that one day our descendants may walk again upon this land."

The Lords rose from the table and reaching out to one another with open arms and full hearts, made their final farewells. Shaken hands lingered long within each grasp and many a gripped shoulder and pummelled back felt the keenness of the touch a good while after. When finally they began to drift towards the door, Aran raised his voice to speak again.

"Whatever path you choose for yourselves and your families, know that my father…" he hesitated, his voice hoarse, "your King, is full of gratitude for your years of service…"

"Our young buck has come of age," whispered Zabian, bending his head towards Methna.

"A natural leader, without doubt," she replied.

"I wish you God's speed on your homeward journey," Aran continued. "Travelling conditions are hard, but I would ask that you send your people who are prepared to fight without delay. For it is here at Kinfallon that the battle for the Northland will be lost or won."

* * * * * *

The Great Hall was growing cold after all the heat and bluster of the day; the fire laying sprawled across the hearth, just a mountain of ash hiding a slumbering heart of gold.

"Morven," Aran raised his eyes and searched her face as they stood together surveying the smouldering embers. "I need to ask you… and Matty…" he glanced across to where Matty stood by the door waiting for her, "to do something for me."

Morven detected something in Aran's look that made her shiver. "I'm not going to like it, am I?" she asked flatly.

"No," he replied, beckoning to Matty to join them.

Morven reached nervously for Matty's hand.

"I believe that you – the two of you should leave for Weyland without delay. It is you who should bear the Snake Sword and lead our people north."

"No, Aran," Morven pleaded, squeezing Matty's hand. "You cannot ask this of us."

"I can," he said firmly; his eyes keen with conviction, "and I do."

The colour in Matty's face slipped away and he sighed. "I thought it might come to this."

"No, no, surely not," Morven shook her brown curls in defiance. "There are plenty of others who would gladly go – gladly go in our place." She laughed nervously. "I see what you do, brother, you wish to spare us. But you cannot believe after all we've been through – that we could leave whilst you remain…"

"Morven, please," he replied. "Think of what we fight for: the hope that we can rid our land of this tyrant and live again as free people. Now I see that we have been fortunate as an island people to have been unmolested for so long. But always the threat from beyond these waters has been great – now we must acknowledge this and act accordingly. Our fighting force should have been bigger and stronger, our borders fortified…"

He paused; his head ached after all the talking of the day and his eyes felt heavy. "Alliances should have been forged with other nations of the Great Crossland – but all this will take time – hopefully work for the future – should God grant us one…"

A faint smile rippled across his lips. "But, in our favour, as always, is the nature of our land: its vastness, its harshness and the stubbornness of our women."

Morven turned her face to Matty as tears tipped from her eyes.

"If you were my brother, Morven," continued Aran, "I would still be standing here making the same request that you give what is left of our family some stake in a future life wherever it may be."

Morven rushed into Aran's arms and her sobs burst upon his shoulder.

Aran held her close and looked to Matty.

"Together, my friend, my brother, you will secure hope for us… though I will miss you by my side for there was never a trial – in all my life – where you did not stand beside me."

31

Kyler raised his head and cocked one ear. Akir watched him rise majestically from his slumber, curb the growl that rattled in his throat, and head off through the awakening forest. She lifted her snout then and sniffed; uncurling her body, she yawned, idly stretched out her limbs, and breaking into a trot followed silently in his tracks.

* * * * * *

The horsemen entered the clearing around Balac's home and stopped. Kamron, accompanied by two of his men, dismounted. One of the two men bent and gathering a large stone from the thawing earth threw it at the door.

Balac stiffened. "Not expecting guests, I take it?"

He slid the wooden panel in the top half of the door a fraction to the right and peered through the slit. "It's Volger's crew."

"How many?" Jesyka asked.

"Eight," he paused. "Including Kamron…"

A second stone thudded against the timbers.

He offered an unconvincing grin and began to draw back the bolts. "I think now would be a good time for you to practise your party trick," he paused, "and disappear."

Once outside he pulled the door shut behind him and stepped away from the cottage.

"What do you want here?" Balac asked.

"Merely a moment of your time," said Kamron, his eye resting upon the closed door. "Do you live alone?"

Balac hesitated before repeating the question. "What do you want here?"

"This is Lord Kamron," said the soldier to Kamron's right, "his father is now ruler of this land." He puffed out his chest and sneered. "And you will address him with due deference or face the consequences."

Again Balac directed his words towards Kamron. "What do you want here?" he paused, inclining his head slightly, "with due deference."

The soldier who had spoken flushed with indignation and, drawing a short sword, took a step closer. Olran, housed in a small paddock at the side of the cabin, began to race about the enclosure, flicking her mane and snorting her displeasure.

"I take it you do not see many people out this way?" asked Kamron, narrowing his eye as he scrutinized Balac.

"That's the way I like it. I have no need for the company of men."

"Or women?" Kamron added. The soldiers grinned.

"My wife is dead. I live alone." Balac was weighing up his chances. Three men on foot and five mounted. Not unsurmountable.

"We are recruiting," Kamron explained. "That is, we are encouraging all able-bodied men to join our ranks. Already our forces march upon the Northland."

"Whatever your cause – it has nothing to do with me."

Kamron sighed. "I thought you might say that, but you are wrong. You are a subject of this land and therefore you are duty bound to do my bidding." Kamron paused. "I'm afraid the smoke," he nodded towards the roof, "rather gave you away."

"And what if I refuse?"

"Well, that's quite simple," offered the man to Kamron's left. "We just persuade you," he said moving forward.

As Balac took a step back, the horses grew uneasy; nostrils flaring and hooves stomping the earth. The rider-less horses began to swing their heads wildly, barring their teeth and rearing up as the three men snatched at the flapping reins.

"God help us, it's those damned wolves again," called one of the mounted riders. "Devils in disguise they are."

Balac suppressed a smile.

"Friends of yours are they?" screeched Kamron, as he grab his horse's reins and swung himself up into the saddle.

"It would appear so," he replied.

The pack stood amongst the trees at the edge of the clearing; their mere presence driving the beasts into a frenzy. As the horses reared and bucked, spinning around with startled eyes, the riders screamed across to one another searching for a way out of the clearing.

Balac raised his fingers to his lips and produced a high-pitched whistle. Akir and Kyler, lifting their heads, drew back a few paces into the forest and sank to the floor. There was a momentary pause before the rest of the pack followed suit.

Kamron, steadying his mount, was breathing heavily. "Impressive," he sneered, his eye flickering with anger. "Useful friends indeed."

"More loyal than the two-footed variety in my experience," Balac replied.

As the horsemen gathered together and made ready to depart, Kamron rode his horse to stand before Balac. Kyler rose to his feet.

"These wolves seem to be making a habit of rescuing people." He paused. "Strange, don't you think?"

Balac remained silent.

"I hope we meet again," Kamron added, "when your friends are not around to save the day."

* * * * * *

Entering the cabin, Balac closed the door and leaning against it exhaled loudly. "Alright, I know you're good at this game – I give in."

Jesyka rose from where she had been sitting on the woodpile; the ghost of a smile playing on her lips as she lifted troubled eyes.

The atmosphere around the cabin remained tense for the rest of the day. They spoke little and busied themselves with mundane everyday tasks: Jesyka tending the fire and producing a plate of vegetable broth; Balac taking himself down to the stream to wash and returning to feed and groom Olran.

When they finally sat opposite each other at the small wooden table to eat, Jesyka knew that the theme of their discussions of late was about to be revisited with vigour.

"Have you not given enough? Will not these guardians that you speak of galvanise a fighting force to action?" Balac raised his eyes from the steaming bowl set before him. "King Broehain betrayed you, and your father and brother are already sacrificed to this cause."

"I have come to understand how King Broehain was caught in an elaborate trap," said Jesyka softly. "For it is the stuff of nightmares to face such a dilemma." She sighed; a slight frown forming across her brow. "In the end he chose to live a lie for four years. And for four years he deceived his own children and a whole nation…" Her face flushed suddenly. "But never forget, that ultimately this was Volger's work."

"And your brother and father?"

"Also Volger's work. And therefore all the more reason to hold true. Whatever the cost, it is my destiny to stand with and for my people."

"The odds are stacked against you – you know this. What is the good of offering false hope?" He laid down his spoon and pushed the bowl away. "Probably worse than none."

She sighed again, sitting back in her chair this time and raising her eyes. "Not false hope," she said. "Grossly outnumbered... possibly." She shrugged.

"Most definitely," he snapped back.

"But this fight is not of our making," she offered in earnest. "If we fight and fail then it will be for someone else in years to come to rise up – knowing our story and in our name – because we stood against this tyranny." Jesyka thought for a moment that she detected a glimmer of consideration in his eyes. "Volger will not hold the Northland on its knees forever."

"Do you really believe men ever learn? Ever stop craving for power over others, only to abuse it having won it?" He searched her face and then dropped his gaze to the soft glow of the fire. "Perhaps in a thousand years things will be different..."

"But until then all that we have is who we are and what we believe in." Jesyka leant forward, attempting to draw him in. "If we hold true to nothing, if we have no belief and no faith in either God or man, what do we live for?"

"But then surely if we do not love, do not care – then we will feel no pain, no loss..."

"And what is the worth of such a life? If we do not live for something, for someone, how are we to live at all? Just to survive – to exist? Eat only to feed a body – then what of the mind, what of the spirit?" She could see his eyes becoming moist. "Balac, if men pull apart from one another, no attachment, no allegiance, then would not the world become even more brutal than it already is?"

He smiled suddenly. "You are so young to have borne so much loss, and yet still you cling to your cause like a great anchor in a storm."

"You are a goodly man, Balac. I cannot accept that you do not hold strong convictions of your own." She reached out across the table with hesitant fingers. "Do you believe in anything?" she asked.

"I believed *I* had a destiny once – to be a husband and a father." He sat back; his eyes beginning to harden. "And then I was persuaded to fight for a cause. My wife's kin drew me into a generation-old dispute over land. So I went with them to fight for their supposedly 'just cause' – but they did not protect my family in my absence – not even her own blood. My wife was killed; my daughter taken and traded oversees."

The muscles grew tense around his jaw. "I tracked the nomadic tribes that I believed held her across the desert lands for two years, but I never found her. So when I reached the coast again, I abandoned her. I tried to convince myself that she was dead and reunited with her mother, because this strangely comforted me. Because I wanted to stop hurting, to stop hoping..."

Jesyka watched his mouth twitch and his nostrils flare as he pulled at the air.

"And now what?" she asked softly. "Will you stay and live out your life with Akir and Kyler? Is that enough?"

She waited.

"Join our fight, Balac. Come north with me," she pleaded.

His eyes seemed to refocus; he spread his hands wide upon the table and stared down at them.

"I cannot help but think that my daughter would have been strong like you – like her mother." He raised his eyes to meet hers. "You have rekindled in me a father's care, a father's love and a desire to see his child thrive. I can do nothing other than encourage you to defy your destiny, because all I long for is that you live… And though I would gladly fight beside you, I cannot be there to see you fall."

Jesyka grabbed at his hands and squeezed them within her own. "How can I ever repay your kindness – for you gave me back my life?" She smiled broadly; blinking back the tears. "Though you made it clear I was not the easiest of patients – for indeed you told me so many times."

Balac laughed loudly. "Indeed, I could have saved myself a great deal of trouble had I left you where you lay within that copse. Though Akir would never have forgiven me – of that I have no doubt."

"Where will you go, when I leave?" she asked.

"I have a mind to return to the desert lands and search again for my daughter, Mia."

"How old will she be?"

"Nearly seven," he sighed.

And withdrawing his hands from her grip he rose to his feet. "Perhaps you will grant me one favour, Jesyka, if you can," he said, looking down at her. "Survive."

* * * * * *

When Jesyka awoke the morning after Kamron's visit, she knew instantly that Balac had gone. Looking around the room at all the familiar items that had been part of her life for the last three months, she raised unsteady fingers to trembling lips. She watched wisps of dark grey smoke curl lazily upwards from the remnants of yesterday's blazing fire. And then the tears came; as she saw that the hammock had gone, only the bent iron hooks standing proud from the cabin's timbers told of what had once been. It was alright to cry, she supposed. After all, there was no one there to see.

These are the last tears, she told herself, the last until the battle for the Northland is done. There was no time, and no merit in feeling sorry for herself beyond this moment; these tears would be all she would allow herself to soothe her pain and lay a layer of acceptance over the here and now.

As the sobs subsided she rose to her feet. She felt strong; her mind embracing the growing awareness that past events, good or ill, would stay forever as silent shadows within her heart. For now she realised that she had no wish to see these spectres gone; for they did not remain to be a burden to drag her down, but a consciousness to lift her up.

Jesyka began to gather her belongings; an urgency quickening her movements as she recalled Kamron's words: *"Already our forces march upon the Northland."*

On opening the door she gasped to see Olran waiting. Olran raised her head and snorted with delight; impatient to be on her way, she pawed at the frost hardened earth.

"Thank you, Balac," Jesyka whispered.

She grinned then; recalling, as she mounted Olran and ran her fingers through her newly brushed mane, how they had disagreed over who should take her.

"It makes no sense for me to take Olran; when I reach the coast I intend to board the first vessel leaving these shores," said Balac.

"She could go with you, you know that," replied Jesyka.

"Yes, but if we could ask her," he pulled a face, "I don't

think that being herded below deck, with terrified livestock awaiting slaughter, would appeal."

She bit her lip then, remembering how they had laughed together for the last time.

Riding away from the cabin, she fixed her eyes on the road ahead, and fought the urge to look back. So that was the end of the matter, she told herself: for she had made her decision and he had made his.

32

On the heels of the receding snow, Volger led the first column of warriors northward at a monotonous pace. The land was awakening only to find itself pounded by the feet of marching soldiers, the hooves of thousands of horses and the hefty lumbering war machines with their inherent soulless rumble.

Volger was glad to be on the move, even if it was at a snail's pace. He had been heartened by his visit south and the realisation that his master plan was now within reach. Though he thought upon it less, the lingering irritation of the unknown whereabouts of the heir plagued him like a recurring itch that would not be satiated. When Kamron eventually arrived on site, having led the final complement of their forces, he found his father standing on the edge of a vast plain looking towards a distant castle upon the hillside.

"Ah, at last," cried Volger, clamping a welcoming arm around his son's shoulders. "Behold. This is it – Kinfallon Castle – stronghold of the Northlanders."

Kamron stared ahead at the expansive stretch of ground, still garnished with opaque patches of ice. "The earth remains frozen here," he observed.

Volger sighed. "Yes, indeed, but it will not be long before we can advance. We have been here three weeks and already the air is warming. Just a matter of days should see the ground fit for men to march upon – and die upon – and yet firm enough to withstand the weight of the sling and the bow."

"Has there been much movement?" asked Kamron, nodding towards the castle.

"There was an apparent sighting of a Northland spy." He shrugged. "It provided a moment of excitement and something for the men to talk about." He paused. "He evaded capture, so I am told, because he was uncommonly fast upon his feet." Volger rolled his eyes. "The sooner we advance the better. Idle men become sluggish."

"When was this?" asked Kamron.

"A few days ago," he offered. "Besides, there would be little they could learn beyond what they see from their own battlements: that we are here – that our numbers are great – that our weaponry is formidable." Volger shrugged again. "And if they were seeking some knowledge of our plan of attack? Well, that is all in here," he smirked, tapping his forehead.

"Apart from that, nothing else to speak of... except, that is," Volger added, thoughtfully, "the lights every night upon the battlements – and the music."

"Music," Kamron turned to look at his father. "You jest?"

"No, indeed, you will hear it for yourself soon enough – strange, haunting sounds – not totally unpleasant. Apparently the Northlanders play some sort of pipes."

Kamron sniggered. "You mean they play music every night?"

"Not just at night, sometimes throughout the day," Volger replied an amused look upon his face.

"And this lot," he raised both arms gesturing to the vast force encamped behind him, "howl and hoot like desert dogs in response."

"A proud and unpredictable people, these Northlanders," offered Kamron.

"Certainly a breed apart from anything else we have encountered. Makes life a tad more interesting," said Volger.

Kamron stole a glance at his father's unusually ruddy complexion. "You appear in exceptionally good spirits, father."

Volger pushed his chest forward, breathing in sharply through his nostrils. "I do not care much for this northern climate – it is too unpredictable. In the course of a single day I have witnessed all manner of twists and turns in the weather – but the air is good here. I doubt I've ever slept better."

He slapped Kamron heartily on the back. "Invigorating," he added, taking another deep breath. "And this will be the jewel that completes the crown – for I have decided that it is there," he raised his arm, motioning with a leather-clad hand towards Kinfallon Castle, "where I intend to be enthroned as Supreme Leader of the Great Crossland."

* * * * * *

Kamron, wishing to acquaint himself with the layout of the camp, whose dimensions were now that of a large rural town, stepped from his tent. Shivering in response to the early evening chill, he swung his cloak about his shoulders and raised the hood.

Volger's men, much experienced in the logistics of warfare, had created a veritable living community: from a bakery, churning out hundreds of loaves a day; to a miniature farm, teeming with all manner of livestock; and thus ensuring that warring stomachs and spirits would never flag for want of sustenance.

The entire force had been split into four units for the purposes of travelling north; but were installed now collectively under a mass of temporary wooden-framed structures covered with lengths of canvas and wool. The first and fourth contingents, led by Volger and Kamron, had consisted of the more seasoned men under their command; whilst the second and third units contained those recently conscripted from Northland's sister nations.

Sandwiching them on the trek north, and housing them at the centre of the site, was aimed at providing scarce opportunity for them to contemplate further acts of defiance. The ease with which these men had been roused to riot, in response to Jesyka's rallying cry, had alarmed Volger; who had ordered that any further sign of dissent was to be dealt with swiftly and harshly.

Kamron had just passed the stabling area when he stopped; turned sharply and retraced his steps to stand before the main paddock. The conspicuous head of a tall pale grey, amongst the varying shades of brown, had summoned his attention.

"That horse," he gestured to the attendant on guard. "Whose horse is that?"

The man lifted his head. "What, my Lord, the grey?"

"Yes, yes," he responded impatiently. "Bring it forward. I want a better look."

The man clambered over the wooden rails that encircled the paddock and lowering himself down amongst the horses pursed his lips and cooed; he crept stealthily through the herd, his eyes fixed upon the dark grey muzzle and silver mane, as he reached for the bridle that hung loose about his shoulder.

"Well, it's no officer's horse," said the man, bending low and squeezing his thin frame back through the gap in the rails, "for they are housed elsewhere."

Kamron pushed back his hood and stared at the grey, as the man tied the reins loosely about the fence post. Stepping closer, Kamron reached out; the horse jerked its head away violently, eyes widening and pupils constricting.

"Easy, easy, girl. Settle now," smoothed the man.

"Well I never," said Kamron under his breath, a flush rising to his face.

"How did this horse get here?" he demanded.

"Er, well…" the man hesitated. "I don't rightly know."

"Then I suggest you find me someone who does."

Kamron paced in front of the grey; his eye never wavering from the beast, as it strained against its bindings: nostrils dilated and dripping moisture.

The man returned at a trot with a shorter, much heavier-built man trying to keep apace close behind.

"This is Gregory, my Lord. He knows about the beast."

Gregory stopped before Kamron and offered a gentle nod; removing his hat, he drew a filthy rag from his coat pocket and dabbed at the perspiration that spotted his brow.

"She wa' found, mi Lord, tethered to a tree some half a mile to the west," said Gregory, his breathing laboured. "Unusual beast – not a common breed – an' sportin' a fancy saddle too she wa'. So, the duty guards gave the dogs the scent an' let em loose." Gregory leant towards Kamron conspiratorially and lowered his voice. "Cos they wa' thinkin' – could be a spy about the camp."

"And?" queried Kamron.

"Well, mi Lord, the dogs wa' fair demented, runnin' every which way howlin' like banshees they wa'." Gregory dabbed again at his forehead. "But there wa' no-one, no-one at all." He paused for effect.

"An' then, there he wa' – appeared outta nowhere, runnin' like the very devil wa' at 'is back – out across the plain headin' straight for the castle."

"Who, damn it? Who was running?"

"Well, the spy, a course. They reckon he must have left 'is horse some way off, thinkin' she'd be safe enough, an' then set about 'is business – snoopin' around – so then, when the dogs got too close for comfort he legged it."

"Was he a tall man, broad with sandy coloured hair?"

"Na, mi Lord, not at all. Nothin' like that. He wa' just a slip of a lad really. In fact, if truth be told, when I saw him runnin' – an' Lord above could he run – I would've wagered, wi' any man, that it wa' a woman."

"Indeed," said Kamron slowly, raising his fingers to press hard against his lips. "And she… he, escaped unharmed?"

"Well, that wa' funniest thing of all – not that we know much about the beasts that lives in these 'ere parts – but, you could have blown me down with a breath of fresh air, when this ruddy big stag – cos I'd never seen one that close up before, an' Lord what a sight he wa' – came thunderin' out across the plain from that there forest to the east."

Gregory became ever more animated, encouraged by his captivated listener. "An' then – right at the back of him came a whole herd of 'em – must have bin fifty – naw probably nearer seventy or more. An' Lord what a racket. So, on they came, stampedin' across the plain an' right across the line of fire – so the archers couldn't see owt. They'd been all set – right on target to bring that runner down – but like I say, no such luck, no luck at all..." He paused for breath. "I surely ain't seen anythin' like it in all my born days. An' they just kept on comin'. So, by the time the last of 'em had passed by – that little slip of a spy wa' nowhere to be seen."

"Did not my father witness this spectacle?" asked Kamron.

"Na, I think not, mi Lord," he frowned, his face red and glowing. "Cos that would be the day he went off to the Isle of Mortonsfayre to see that old Abbey. I did hear say that they hadn't realised it wa' a tidal causeway an' ended up spendin' the night." Gregory chuckled and then stopped abruptly. "Sorry, mi Lord, no offence intended."

"Well, Gregory, that was most enlightening," said Kamron, hooking a finger into the collar of his cloak and pulling the cloth away from his perspiring skin. "I've a fancy for the beast; have it brought to my quarters in the morning."

"Will do, mi Lord. I'll see to that personally," said Gregory, replacing his hat.

Kamron backed away from the horse, still struggling to let him out of his sight. When he finally turned his back, there was a discernible spring in his step as he moved swiftly through the camp. Rubbing damp palms together, he lowered his head, concealing the grin that stretched across his face.

33

"I doubt I would have survived without him – indeed I owe him a great debt." said Jesyka.

"From what you describe – a troubled man – who has suffered much," replied Methna. "And so he turns away from the world of men," she sighed. "I, for one, would not judge him too harshly for that."

"Let me guess," Aran feigned a puzzled expression. "Surely not more talk about the wonderful Balac." He strode across the sun-streaked floor of his father's old chamber to stand before Methna and Jesyka as they sat upon the great sill of the window that looked out to the south.

Offering an overly low bow, he raised laughing eyes to meet hers. "But truly," he said, the levity suddenly slipping from his face. "We all owe him a great debt – I would thank him with all my heart for restoring you to us…"

Methna cleared her throat. "And now you must excuse me whilst I climb those endless stairs, yet again, to try and entice Torpen to leave Kinfallon. His stubbornness is beyond all reason; indeed I hold little hope of persuading him."

As the door closed behind her, Aran filled the vacant seat.

"And yet," Aran stated, "it gives me no pleasure to think that he has restored you only for you to fall here…"

Jesyka turned to look south and rest her eyes upon the

dark mass of Volger's army that clung to the edge of the plain like a venomous leech. She shivered.

"Why does he wait?" she mused.

"Who knows the workings of such a mind," Aran replied, following her gaze.

A gentle silence settled about them, as, for a few moments, they drifted away into their own thoughts.

"I am sorry to have missed Morven and Matty," said Jesyka eventually, "but I am glad that you succeeded in persuading them to go. And what of your mother and father?"

"They have also gone north. I discovered they had formed a notion to take their own lives should Volger be victorious." He sighed. "My mother would never allow herself to be taken alive again… And it is now my father who appears to have the more broken mind." He hesitated. "But I felt sure they would leave if Morven accompanied them – and so it proved."

"And your mother – does she know you now as her son?" Jesyka asked.

"I believe she does, but…" he paused, "I believe there is much she would like to say but somehow cannot form the words – cannot allow what she truly feels to be heard by anyone – not even herself. I sense that she fears being overwhelmed – that she may lose control and never regain it." He breathed deeply. "So she remains affable but at the same time somehow detached. Indeed, I cannot even make out if she has forgiven my father or merely tolerates him – he fusses around her like a doting handmaid and she lets him – responding with a firm sort of kindness."

"Her suffering cannot be imagined – four years…" Jesyka raised her eyes.

She could not help but detect subtle changes in his face over the few months they had been apart; not just the scars, but calmer, knowing eyes. Indeed his whole demeanour heralded the message that the boy had become a man.

"So you predict that we will fall?" she asked, resurrecting his earlier comment. "And that there will be no future for us?"

"I do not dwell upon it – for I am not by nature a melancholy man," he smiled. "But I cannot help but think that there is perhaps no way out for us…"

Jesyka looked thoughtful. "Did you ever in your mind's eye picture yourself as a father?"

"Strangely, I have thought upon it recently." He laughed. "And what about you, did you envisage being a mother?" He laughed again. "A grandmother, even?"

"We are in danger of wandering into the realms of fantasy," she replied. "For our futures would never have been left to our own design. Whilst I returned to the Northland to fulfil my destiny as heir to your people – you are also bound by who you are. Your call is also to serve, to give of yourself for others. Different titles we may have – but a common purpose all the same."

"At least we always knew that this day might come; but the others, the thousands who must accompany us on this journey – I would spare them this fight if I could." He dropped his eyes.

"I thought you said you were not a melancholy man?" Jesyka swung her legs down from the sill and faced into the room. "I am not sure I believe you. I have met many a Northlander who is prone to excessive brooding. I begin to think it is a national trait." She threw him a teasing glance. "I'll bet you are about to tell me that at least we have some hope – and that is to die well." She jumped down from her perch and turned to face him.

"Aahh," he grinned, his eyes glistening, "and I do not believe you – for you once told me that you did not read minds." He eased himself from his seat and standing before her reached for her hand. "And yet *that* is exactly what I was about to say."

As Jesyka raised her face to his the door burst open and Nunca filled the space. "Come, there is movement – men on horseback bearing a white flag."

* * * * * *

"This is not Volger's way. I do not like it," uttered Zabian, his dark eyes smouldering. "Something strange is afoot."

Jesyka, Aran, Methna and the guardians stood upon the battlements and watched as a group of Volger's riders approached the centre of the plain and stopped. There were six men in total and as two of them took a few paces forward and removed their ornate gleaming helmets, it was evident that Kamron and Volger were amongst them.

"What can their game be?" muttered Choi.

"I doubt we'll find out unless we ask," said Jesyka.

"I agree," offered Methna, her eyes narrowing as she stared ahead. "I can see little choice, other than to ride out and meet them."

"The rest of their troops are too far back to cause a problem," Nunca shrugged. "The risk is minimal."

"So six of them, and six of us," said Aran.

"That's the measure of it," said Zabian. "Sounds like a match made in heaven."

* * * * * *

"I will speak, father," said Kamron. "If you are in agreement?" he quickly added.

Volger cleared his throat; the muscles in his face appeared taut. "This is your proposal. Indeed, I am still unsure of its worth." Situated on his son's blind side, he turned to stare at the dappled skin and scowled.

"As we discussed," added Kamron, eagerly, "there is nothing to lose on our part and all to gain."

"Yes," murmured Volger. "So you said, many times. But you cannot be sure that she is even here."

"Well, we will see soon enough," he replied, his cheeks suddenly colouring. "Here they come."

Hundreds of archers raced along the battlements taking up their positions, as they watched the Northlanders exit the castle gate, pass through the gatehouse and head out across the plain at a gentle canter to meet their foe.

Volger lifted his chin and stretched out his neck, clamping his teeth together until they ached. "And to think," he hissed. "They were all my prisoners once – apart from…" He raised a cupped hand to shield his eyes from the brightness of the day as he watched the riders approach.

"So the heir lives," snorted Volger, "as you predicted. But who is the other woman, with a head of golden curls?"

"Probably Methna," Kamron replied.

"Ah," Volger smirked, curling his lip, "the merry widow."

Jesyka and Aran rode side by side, flanked on Jesyka's right by Methna and Zabian, and on Aran's left by Choi and Nunca. The riders eased their pace to a trot as they grew closer, stopping some fifteen feet short of Volger and Kamron.

"Greetings, Northlanders," began Kamron. "So we finally meet again."

When no response came, Kamron cleared his throat and continued. "You have no doubt assessed the strength of our forces and come to the inevitable conclusion that our victory is assured."

"This being the case," said Aran, "what is your purpose here?"

"Where is King Broehain?" snapped Volger.

"Indisposed," answered Aran curtly. "You will deal with me."

"Indeed," stated Volger, raising an eyebrow.

Kamron cleared his throat noisily. "We come to offer a possible alternative to war," he stated. "We propose an alliance."

"Do I look like a fool?" Aran replied, shaking his head in disbelief. "Or do you suspect that I have taken leave of my senses?"

"What I do suspect is that you would wish to avoid loss of life amongst your subjects and to have some say in the future governance of your land. Neither of which is likely if you choose to rebuff this one and only offer of a negotiated peace." Kamron replied curtly.

"A negotiated peace," Aran spat the words back at him. "Nothing could hold our two people as one. Indeed you can propose nothing that could ever make this possible."

"I propose a marriage," said Kamron.

"Dear God," muttered Methna to Zabian. "I cannot believe what I have just heard."

Aran's face grew rigid. "And who did you have in mind? My sister?"

"No, indeed, you misunderstand me." Kamron finally allowed his gaze to fall upon Jesyka.

"Your family will be permitted to reign here and govern this land, under our jurisdiction of course," Kamron's voice began to betray his excitement. "For my father will be Supreme Ruler over all the Great Crossland and as his son if I were to be united with the only remaining heir of the Tribe of Skea then we could bring peace and prosperity to all four nations."

Kamron's horse grew restless and shook its silver mane.

"Life is full of surprises, my little friend," whispered Nunca to Choi. "I did not see that one coming."

"Well?" roared Volger, when no immediate response came.

"Father," hissed Kamron. "They may wish to consider…"

"No," said Aran, a menacing tone entering his voice, "we do not."

Though the colour had drained from her face, Jesyka's amber eyes were ablaze.

"We thank you for your offer," said Aran, coldly "but we must refuse…"

"Let Jesyka speak for herself," screeched Kamron, his eye blinking repeatedly.

"Let it go, my son," said Volger. "This whole spectacle has shamed us enough. We will have our revenge on the battlefield."

Jesyka's breathing grew shallow. "You who murdered my brother and my father – you would ask this of me?" Tilting her head back and raising her eyes heavenward, her shoulders began to shake and then the laughter, coarse, unearthly laughter burst from her.

"Rise up, Olran. Rise my beauty!" she cried.

At the sound of her voice, Olran instantly dropped her head, kicked out her back legs and reared up sharply; delivering a high-pitched scream she pawed at the air with her forelegs. Kamron was thrown forward and then swiftly backwards, flinging him from his saddle to sprawl upon the earth. He scrambled to his feet, his face puce with fury as he grabbed at the whip at his belt.

"Run, Olran. Run!" screamed Jesyka.

Olran lurched forward; with swishing tail and flowing mane she swerved around the Northlanders and raced away across the plain.

"You have your answer," said Aran.

Though his eyes never left Volger's horrified expression, Zabian emitted a clicking noise as he coaxed his horse to back away: the others immediately following his lead.

"And I will have my revenge!" Kamron roared. "There will be no mercy, no mercy for anyone..."

"Now we see your true colours," called Aran. "Now we see the father's son. Mercy is not in your nature so I do not expect it. And to surrender is not in mine so do not expect that either."

* * * * * *

"A proposal of marriage," pondered Methna, as they rode back through the gatehouse. "I can scarce believe it even now."

Jesyka smiled weakly; a look of confusion clouding her face. "What should we make of this strange episode, mother?"

"I cannot say," replied Methna, shaking her head. "Though it causes great unease, for we felt we had some measure of Volger – and yet this twist by Kamron shows even greater unpredictability – or mere madness."

Choi following close behind turned in his saddle to speak with Nunca. "Perhaps it was that blow to the head," said Choi thoughtfully. "For there's no telling what that can do to a man."

"With the obvious problem being," replied Nunca with a frown, "that I did not hit him hard enough."

Zabian had stopped half way up the roadway and waited until Aran was beside him.

"Of course, Volger only has the one son to leave his dynasty to," said Zabian. "Perhaps it flattered him to think that his lineage could include the heir of the Tribe of Skea – which until now he has spent all his time trying to erase." He sighed. "Though I do not believe he was in complete agreement with this course of action."

"Maybe the whole proposal was nothing more than it seems," offered Aran. "Kamron is obsessed – is desperate to keep her alive – and the only way he can get his father to even contemplate the idea, is to find a vantage point and fight his corner as best he can." Aran shrugged. "But I agree with you. I do not think Volger was a willing party in that spectacle. And now he is all the more dangerous having seen his son refused."

"True, but I venture he is secretly pleased with the outcome and will therefore act immediately," said Zabian.

Aran stared out across the plain towards Volger's camp. "And Kamron – will he give up on this notion?"

Zabian shook his head. "Somehow I think not."

Shrill sounding horns blasted their uneasy squall out across the plain as a multitude of eager warriors bellowed in response.

"I think we can safely say that the talking is over," said Zabian, urging his horse forward.

34

Volger's advancing force smothered the vast plain; the menacing beat of their progress ringing keen upon the damp cool air. Accompanied by the roar of thousands, a dozen war engines were dragged through the ranks and bullied into place at the front of the assembled mass.

For two hours, without respite, the mighty catapults winged their cargo of rocks against the outer wall of the castle compound; with some of the missiles weighing over one hundred pounds, the merciless pounding soon provoked fractures to run like rivers across the beaten stone. Then it was the turn of the torsion-powered bows; firing spears whose shafts were strengthened with beaten metal straps and armour-plated heads, they drove deep into the widening ruptures. It was only a matter of time before the battlements began to crumble, as a series of rubble-spewing cascades began to flow down the hillside: each one accompanied by the rapacious hollering of the enemy below.

To the east, where the castle gatehouse stood, Kamron was overseeing the battering of the gatehouse door. The roadway which led up from the plain below was initially broad with a steadily growing incline; halfway along it narrowed significantly to a width accommodating no more than four horsemen riding abreast. On either side of this constricted section, untamed terrain fell sharply away: its jagged rocks and sparse vegetation making it a haven for birds of prey and grim-faced weasels.

"Why is this door not breached?" yelled Kamron. "There has been more than ample time." Kamron glared at the backs of the men who charged repeatedly, thrashing the ram against the gatehouse door. He sat astride a majestic chestnut steed, with a heavy black mane and tail, who fidgeted and fretted upon the narrow coarse-way.

The red-faced officer conducting operations looked up. "Can't make it out, my Lord," he gasped. "We're through the wood – but there seems to be something else…" He bent his knees and crouching down peered beneath the protective hood of the battering ram, to view his men's handiwork. "They've riveted something to the back of the door," he shouted. "It looks like a sheet of metal. It's hardly dinted." He straightened himself, a puzzled expression upon his face.

"The defence wall to the south is already falling and you can't even break down this door," he roared. "Bring up Goliath."

"The way is too narrow, my Lord, and the angle too steep."

"Then bring ramps wide enough to bear it and blocks to level it, man!" screamed Kamron. "Do it, now."

Narrow, spiral steps curled upwards, buried deep within each of the two towers that formed the outer structure of the gatehouse; upon both staircases four men crouched in the darkness, listening and waiting. Creeping through the newly built roof space, from one gatehouse tower to the other, Choi made his final checks.

* * * * * *

Eight pairs of hefty war horses began to drag the colossal battering ram, Goliath, up towards the gatehouse; as a chorus of raucous shouts and cheers rose from the heavily armed foot soldiers who followed on behind. The journey proved arduous for the team, their burden uncommonly heavy; as two handlers, walking either side of the lead pair, held their bridles and spoke encouragingly into their ears. On approaching the specially constructed ramp, whose width widened the track by overhanging the precipitous drop on either side by some four feet, they slowed the team to a gentler pace.

The unexpected change in the terrain: to the smooth, pliable timbers that creaked and groaned under the load, caused instant unease amongst the beasts. Whilst the lead pair, with heads bowed, remained focused upon their task, those at the rear, without the benefit of constant reassurance, began to shake their heads and whinny as their anxiety grew.

The horse on the left of the seventh pair suddenly kicked back, clattering his hooves against the rail that divided him from sultry bay directly behind. The startled bay slipped and stumbled, as Goliath swung a fraction to the left. The handler on the left-hand side glared anxiously over his shoulder and pursed his lips.

Many within the endless column of men that continued to snake its way up from the plain grew impatient, as the ascent continued to prove agonisingly slow and the earlier damp air had been replaced by persistent rain.

"Get that horse steadied," yelled a voice from behind.

"Steady it yourself," the handler bellowed back; blood filling his face.

Much to the handler's alarm, the burly-framed man took him at his word, and began to manoeuvre his bulk along the edge of the ramp. Passing Goliath's wheels which stretched beyond the man's height, he grabbed the skittish horse's bridle with his left hand and raised his short sword in his right.

The handler glowered over his shoulder. "No, you imbecile!" he cried.

"I'll get this lot moving," the man growled, paying the handler no heed, as he brought the flat of the sword down sharply upon the rump of the horse.

The horse screamed and swung its hip out to the side banging against the man's torso and causing him to slip. As he clung on to the bridle, the horse's neck was dragged downward at an unnatural angle, yanking the parallel shaft between itself and the horse directly ahead. Becoming instantly alarmed, as its back legs buckled under the force of the unexpected pressure, the beast in front began neighing frantically as it attempted to right itself.

"Dear God!" roared the handler.

Goliath's great wheels stuttered, stopped and then began to roll gently backwards.

"Swing to the front," called out the handler to his counterpart on the right, as he swung his back to the gatehouse, grabbed the bridle on both sides of the horse's head and threw his weight backwards. Digging in with his heels, he found himself slipping upon the damp timbers as his fellow handler followed suit and they strained together to remedy the sliding apparatus.

As instant panic rippled through the column, the soldiers positioned directly behind the reversing war machine began to scream and curse, as they pushed erratically backwards. Instantly those closest to the edge were shoved off into the abyss, by the swell of bodies jostling for space upon the narrow roadway.

Men who found themselves propelled towards oblivion grabbed at their fellow warriors, resulting in groups of men tumbling together to their deaths upon the unrelenting rocks below. The more quick-witted took the option of dropping to the ground and lowering themselves over the edge to hang by their fingertips until the horror was over; however they remained vulnerable to the footfalls of terrified soldiers who trampled unwittingly upon fingers that became bloodied and broken till they could hold no more.

Kamron, watching from the plain below, grew apoplectic with rage. His mouth opened and closed as he screamed upwards to those ensconced in the fiasco, spittle flowing from his gaping mouth: but no one heard. As the handlers fought on and the incline began to lessen, Goliath finally came to a staggering halt.

The handler, his eyes bloodshot and streaming, gestured to his partner to hold his horse's bridle whilst he made his way back towards the skittish horse who stood head bowed, breathing heavily. The burly man, who had managed to cling on to the horse's bridle, was back on his feet, his forehead pressed against the horse's neck.

As he looked up, he was just in time to see the handler's whip come slicing down upon his forearm. He yelped in agony, releasing his grip. The second flick flashed through the air and drove deep across his cheek; as the third and fourth despatched him unceremoniously over the edge. He uttered no sound as he fell, staring up with horror-stricken eyes at his assailant who watched with grim satisfaction.

"Idiot," muttered the handler, turning away.

* * * * * *

As the afternoon wore on the sky appeared to descend towards the siege, as feathery clouds thickened and turned grey. Though the southern wall continued to crumble, now exposing the inner workings of rubble, still it held. Volger sat upon a stallion of jet black; a crimson cape was draped about his shoulders, and the hood, raised against the endless rain, sheltered a thunderous scowl beneath.

"How goes it here, father," said Kamron, drawing his horse to a halt before him.

"Look at that," Volger gestured towards the wall, "ever seen such a depth?"

Kamron frowned.

"We are concentrating on removing the height. When the battlements drop by another few feet I will send men forward. We need to see beyond that wall before the light fades." Volger paused. "And the gatehouse?" He turned his full gaze upon Kamron.

"Goliath is pounding the door as we speak. The original ram could not break it."

"Ha," Volger snorted a derisory laugh, "and where are they?" he screeched. "Not one Northlander seen the whole day long as we pound at their door – our men breaking their backs... Where are they?"

"We will see the whites of their eyes soon enough, father. And when we do – we shall see them wracked with fear."

* * * * * *

Goliath stood before the gatehouse door; its rear, having been raised to bring the machine level, was supported by blocks of wood, rocks, and perspiring men. As the ropes were drawn taut and then released, the boom began to swing. The soldiers remained eerily quiet as they concentrated on the intricate balancing act they were tasked with undertaking.

With the growing momentum, the giant gleaming head, fashioned in the shape of a ram's head, quickly obliterated the already damaged wood to reveal more of the metal beneath. A series of rhythmic cheers, each one louder than the one before, rang through the air; as the heavily pitted steel began to warp and the holding rivets squealed under the strain. But still the door held.

"They will be through any minute," yelled Choi above the din from outside. "But you must await my command."

The walls of the gatehouse were beginning to shift as the beat of the ram shook the structure to its very core and the men inside cowered beneath plumes of crumbling sandstone.

"Hold steady," said Choi.

When the door finally broke from its moorings, the hinges, so well anchored to the stone, carried part of the wall with them. Like the felling of a mighty oak, the door hesitated for a moment before toppling backwards and crashing to the earth: unleashing a cloud of dust that rose high into the air.

"Move into place," called Choi.

The Northlanders shook the sandstone from their hair and clothes and scrambled up into the roof space. The first two headed directly to the far end of the gatehouse and away from the fallen door: whilst the rest positioned themselves at intervals along its length.

With bestial howls of joy, Volger's men rushed forward, squinting to see through the billowing dust to the castle entrance, a mere sixty feet beyond the gatehouse. Those holding Goliath in place held firm, as others, eager to advance, scrambled through the interior of the machine, or round the edge, to jump down gleefully upon the felled door and race on towards the bigger prize ahead.

"Now," yelled Choi, as the two men at the back freed the chains which held a hidden portcullis. Though a dozen soldiers were already beyond the gatehouse, the portcullis dropped with astonishing speed to slam into the ground and halt the rest. At the clamour of the rapidly unfurling chains, the lead warriors swung round, to find to their amazement that they stood alone upon the exposed roadway.

As the tide of bodies continued to rush forward, pressing those at the front up against the portcullis, the gatehouse began to fill.

"Retreat!" they cried. "Go back. Go back. The way is barred."

"Now," yelled Choi again. The Northlanders hauled open vast shutters and peered down at the mayhem below. Amongst the chaos and confusion, one or two of Volger's men glanced up and witnessed the ceiling being drawn back: with perplexed expressions, they strained their necks, to stare into the cavernous pit.

Directly above the felled door, Choi leapt onto the wooden beam that straddled the open space. He ran the length of the gatehouse roof, with a razor-sharp blade in each hand, splicing through the ropes which hung on either side. The action took a matter of seconds and yet the result was devastating: as a maelstrom of rocks fell from a plethora of nets which hung in the darkness.

* * * * * *

"Have we underestimated our foe?" asked Volger grimly, stuffing his mouth with handfuls of moist chicken.

"They obviously used the winter to prepare well," replied Kamron, pacing the floor of his father's tent, as the rain thundered down.

"These guardians, full of trickery from their own lands… And yet I would bet good gold that they command less than a quarter of the force we hold." Volger gathered the skin and bones from his plate and threw them on the fire where they hissed and sizzled.

"Eventually they will run out of tricks and then they will have to face us," said Kamron.

"Come, eat," called Volger, gesturing to Kamron to join him at the table.

"Two days, two backbreaking days it took to bring that wall down a mere six feet and what do we find?" Volger crammed more chicken into his mouth as he stared ahead, "A second wall and a spear-filled gully." He gathered more debris from his plate and this time flung it upon the floor, where the dogs pounced, snapping and snarling at one another with slavering jowls. "And that damned witchery at the gatehouse – took an eternity to clear…"

Kamron, sitting opposite his father, picked at his food. "Perhaps we shall have to burn them after all," he said, lifting his gaze to watch his father's reaction.

Volger sighed and sat back in his chair. "Without doubt a favourite of mine, but…" he picked with grease covered fingers at the meat stuck between his teeth, "I wanted Kinfallon intact." He swung forward and thrashed the table with his fist. "I wanted to be enthroned in their Great Hall, to sleep upon King Broehain's bed and to feed Lord Aran to the crows from his own battlements. And as for Jesyka…"

"No, father," interrupted Kamron darkly. "You must grant me my own revenge upon the heir."

Volger stared at his son, who was rubbing at his temples with trembling fingers. "Quite right, my son, I am sure you will think of something suitably public and entertaining for we must crush this emblem of hope before their very eyes. Break her spirit and in turn we will break the spirit of every Northlander."

"At this rate the siege is likely to endure beyond weeks, possibly months – but if we burn…" Kamron continued to push the food around his plate. "Besides, why not use the Abbey at Mortonsfayre for your enthronement. It is the equal of Iola, is it not? Indeed, you said so yourself."

Volger pulled a large circular plate towards himself upon which sat a hefty game pie whose shiny golden brown crust shone in the glow of the candlelight. He thrust a dagger deep into its centre and hewed himself a wedge. Dragging the back of his hand across his mouth he removed the drips of chicken fat from his lips.

"This infernal weather," said Volger, "will hamper our efforts. Already the slings and bows are stuck in the mud." He took a bite of the aromatic pie and began to chew, his head gently nodding as if in rhythm with his masticating jaws.

"We would need to move the machines closer to shorten the range. Built into the hillside the castle is more formidable than I had imagined…" said Kamron.

"Yes, yes, and this is the problem." Volger looked up wide-eyed, his mouth still full of food. "Our progress from the Southland, though not without pockets of resistance, was never as challenging as these damned Northlanders." Volger swallowed and reached again for the pie. "And this damnable rain. Have you ever seen the like before?"

"As I was saying, father, regarding the burning. We must ensure that the fireballs can reach beyond both outer walls to fall within the compound. For I would venture that many of the inner structures will be made of wood."

Kamron stopped rubbing his temples and lifted his gaze to meet his father's. Volger grabbed the rim of the plate that held the pie and shoved it the length of the table.

"Eat, Kamron. You cannot fight a war on an empty stomach," Volger glared, "nor on revenge alone – for it will eat you first well before the day of reckoning has dawned."

The flicker of a smile crept along Kamron's thin lips. He cut a sizeable wedge from the remaining pie and, lifting it with both hands, stole a hasty glance towards his father, before sinking his teeth into the crust.

Volger sat back in his chair, threw his own plate upon the floor and grinned as he watched the dogs devour the contents and fight over the scraps that lay scattered about.

35

Zabian strode through shallow puddles of rainwater that nestled in the pitted stone of the battlements. He could see Methna and Nunca peering across the boggy plain through the fading light of the day.

"Something interesting?" called Zabian.

"I would say so," replied Nunca. "They are laying ramps – presumably they are planning to move the machines closer."

"Which means they are giving up on breaking through the outer walls and aiming now at causing chaos within," said Methna. "Volger grows impatient. Will it be rocks, I wonder?"

"Or will it be fire?" mused Zabian.

"I doubt we will have long to wait," said Nunca. "Either way, perhaps the time has come to finish this contest."

Methna shivered. "Do you feel that sudden chill upon the air? I think that bog may be as hard as stone come the morning."

Zabian raised an arm and hung it loosely about Methna's shoulders. "That being the case," he said, "then Nunca could be right. The time is nigh to see this business done."

* * * * * *

Though it was still one hour before dawn, Kinfallon Castle was alive with activity. The weapon store within the Great

Hall was much depleted: with all the available weaponry having been distributed to the three thousand who stood expectantly within the castle compound. As Methna predicted, a harsh frost, perhaps the last to grace the early spring weather, gripped the Northland and converted the mud-lashed plain to a pockmarked carpet of iron.

The people appeared no less than euphoric; their spirits having risen each and every day as Volger's attempts to storm the castle had been rebuffed. Some of the Northlanders had laden themselves with so many weapons that they would struggle to march, let alone fight, and had had to be gently persuaded to shed some of their load.

Methna wore the breastplate which bore the silver bear, and the blades forged by Yorcum hung at her waist and across her back: holding back her golden hair was a band of white fur. She joined the guardians to mingle with the Northlanders as they waited for the dawn.

The sheath at Nunca's shoulder was heavy with arrows; and where a leather strap criss-crossed around his waist, two axes hung, concealed beneath his blanket of red and black. Choi, whose usual sombre tones allowed him to flit unseen within the shadows, emerged wearing a scarlet sash which crossed over his shoulders and wrapped repeatedly around his torso. Within this sash a multitude of blades and razor-sharp throwing irons were nestled into his body. In a quiet solitary ritual Choi had painstakingly inserted and memorised the whereabouts of every piece of weaponry.

Zabian threaded his way through the crowd to stand beside Choi.

"I see you mean business today, my friend," he commented, raising an eyebrow as he perused Choi's scarlet attire.

Choi dropped his eyes and smiled. "Likewise, by the shine upon those damnable boots of yours."

Zabian threw back his head and laughed.

Jesyka and Aran walked from the castle to a joyous cheer from the Northlanders who clattered their weapons and surged forward to greet them. Jesyka mounted the trestle table from the Great Hall which had been dragged outside for the occasion.

And then the chanting began. It started at the back of the crowd and swept forward until a deafening crescendo filled the air.

"Jes-y-ka, Jes-y-ka, Jes-y-ka…"

Jesyka reddened and turned her grinning face to Aran. He leapt to join her upon the table top, smiled and bowed: causing jubilant hoots and howls from the mass. Jesyka's hair was scrapped back and her braided amber tresses tethered with a leather thong at the base of her neck; wisps of hair fell forward and framed her face as she raised both arms in a bid to be heard above the din. Finally silence settled upon the scene.

"I offer your no platitudes," she began. "No predictions or falsehoods for they would be an insult to the enormity of the task which is upon us." She paused as she located Methna in the crowd.

"We did not fashion or court this fight. But it is here. It beats now upon our door. And it is led by a man who seeks to eradicate who we are, the tenor of our race, the very nature of the lives we live…" She strode upon the table, her gaze falling upon the faces raised to greet her.

"And for what? What is it that Volger fights for? For wealth? For prestige? For land? To be revered and feared amongst men?" Jesyka shrugged. "Perhaps he desires to be loved? Perhaps he is but a madman?" Laughter rippled through the throng.

"But what we do know is that he has plundered our sister nations, here in the Great Crossland, and it is the Northland alone which now stands against him."

She breathed deeply as silence fell again. "And what we do *not* speculate upon – because we know – is what we fight for." She eased out her shoulders and lifted her head high.

"I stand here as your heir of the Tribe of Skea – and Lord Aran as your future King – and what we offer is all that we have." Jesyka waited until she felt Aran's presence beside her. "Which is ourselves." A roar rose to the heavens accompanied by the first hint of light creeping over the horizon.

"We offer our lives to you – to this land – to this cause – and to our kin – that small band that has sailed away from all that it loves and cares for to carry some hope of a future for our people. And so we fight today for one another," Jesyka reached forward with outstretched arms, "for you, and you, and you… May God give us courage – courage to hope – and if all else fails then courage to die well." She glanced towards Aran and smiled.

"Look to your fellowman and fight with all that you have. You have not lived this life alone and neither will you fight or die alone. For you will be in the best company that a body can muster." Jesyka's eye caught upon Choi's scarlet attire and Zabian's gentle smile.

"So whether we find ourselves above or below the earth, when this day is done, we shall, for all time, be amongst those who we would call, family, friend, and forever Northlander."

They cheered again and rattled their weapons. At the back of the crowd Jesyka could see that Nunca was soothing the impatient Olran, running his fingers through her mane.

"They will speak well of us. Remember us. Our story will pass down from generation to generation. Children will sing songs about how we fought against tyranny – fought against those who would strive to bend our backs to their will, break our spirit and crush our soul." Jesyka struggled to contain the tears as she allowed herself one more glance at Methna.

"Though we are small in number, let us be ferocious in defending that which is ours. Let us honour the mighty stag," she thumped a clenched fist upon her breastplate, "glorious throughout all his days. For when the sun sets upon this land we will walk with him still, through these forests, across these hills and out upon this plain."

36

"Father, come, the war machines are ablaze. They are frozen to the ground but they are afire," called Kamron, bursting into Volger's tent and finding his father seated at the table about to eat breakfast.

Volger stared with incredulity at Kamron, before rushing from the table and following him outside. Twelve great fires, spewing smoke and flames into a glorious blue sky, engulfed the giant slings and bows.

"What the devil…" roared Volger.

"And the Northlanders, they march upon us," cried Kamron. "Can you believe such madness?"

Volger grabbed at Kamron's arms and swung him round to face him. "What is going on, Kamron?"

"The men went out just before dawn to manoeuvre the machines onto the ramps but the ground was frozen and the machines could not be moved." Kamron breathed heavily. "Then the pipes struck up, those damned infernal pipes, and archers filled the battlements. Like ants they said maybe a thousand strong and they fired at the machines with blazing arrows until the ramps and machines were ablaze."

"They march," cried Volger, "you said they march upon *us*?"

"Yes, father, they do. The gates of Kinfallon Castle lay open and the Northlanders are on the march."

Torpen stepped back from the window; where he had stood for some time watching the war machines burn. He shuffled round his circular room and stepped out onto the balcony which hung directly above the eastern entrance. With the colossal timber and metal studded doors standing open, he found himself staring down upon the steady column of mounted and marching Northlanders progressing down the narrow roadway to the plain below.

"Dear Lord, Ferneth," he sighed. "I wish I could still wield a sword and be of some service. Rather than fret away up here worrying about all the young folk." He reached down and patted Ferneth's head. "If only I could do *something…*"

A curious expression crossed his face, as he retraced his steps back into the room. A deepening frown developed above eyes lost in thought, as he made his way towards a pile of discarded books that lay teetering upon the edge of the table.

"I wonder…" he muttered; as he began to flick through the pages with unsteady gnarled fingers. "I wonder…"

* * * * * *

The huge mass of Volger's force surged forward across the frozen ground like a great sea of swaying crimson. The fires had fallen to half their original height and the sky hung bright and clear overhead.

To the west Volger and Kamron sat upon their mounts, with a small number of attendants gathered about them. They had settled upon a small copse, situated upon a gentle grassy hillside, from which to survey the scene below. Staring down, as the opposing forces advanced towards one another,

Kamron bit at his lower lip as he sat hunched forward in his saddle.

"Better odds than I predicted," said Volger.

"I doubt we have seen all," replied Kamron. "I feel sure they will be holding something in reserve."

Volger shrugged, appearing to ignore the comment, as his lip began to curl. "Look at their line; they are too thin, too thin by far," he snorted. "This is the hour. At last the day has come. We will be through them like a knife through butter."

* * * * * *

"Easy does it! Hold the line!" yelled Zabian.

At a canter, a thousand Northlanders moved beyond the burning fires: five hundred abreast and two deep. Zabian rode at the centre; Aran to the left and Methna to the right.

"Await my signal! Hold steady!" Zabian roared.

As those leading the crimson horde of foot soldiers saw the small number of riders that opposed them, they bellowed orders for their troops to increase their speed. Zabian raised his hand and the Northlanders drew to a halt. The horses snorted noisily and pawed at the ground which shook to the rapid irregular beat of the many thousands of feet hurrying towards them.

"Retreat beyond the fires!" bellowed Zabian. "Retreat. Retreat."

Volger's men began to hoop and cheer as they saw the Northlanders swing their mounts about and head back towards the castle wall; the sight of the fleeing horsemen appearing to exert an irresistible urge amongst the advancing troops to lift their speed once more.

At the gallop, the Northlanders covered the ground quickly; again they passed the burning war engines and piles of charred timbers which had toppled from the skeletal remains of the blackened machines. As they grew close to the broken battlements, Zabian drew his double-edged scimitar, and raising it above his head, drew circular movements in the air.

"Turn," he commanded. "Turn and form the line."

As the Northlanders slackened their speed, and turned once more to face the enemy, they formed an arc: the two ends of the line curving back to reach the rubble which remained in towering heaps against the castle wall.

"Dismount," Zabian commanded. And as they leapt from their mounts the frantic peal of a deep-throated bell rang out from Kinfallon. The horses, trained to the sound, instantly sped from the field of battle.

Within the manmade arc, a thousand more Northlanders rose from the ground where they had waited upon bended knee with their shields standing proud before them. The sudden movement of so much newly forged metal being raised to meet the morning sun drew flashes of brilliant white light to streak through the air.

As the Northlanders howled their defiance at the crimson sea that swept ever closer, Jesyka stood at the front of the newly formed arch, eased her broadsword from the scabbard at her back and raised it heavenward. With only a hundred feet of hardened earth standing between the two forces, Volger's men thundered on, encircling the arc and bearing down upon it.

As Nunca rose to stand on top of the crumbling battlements, some five hundred archers clambered into view beside him. Digging their heels into the mountain of loose rubble, they slid through the debris, positioning themselves across the incline, directly above the two thousand Northlanders on the plain beneath them. Beyond the spear-filled gully, a slight figure in black and scarlet raced along the higher inner wall, where five hundred more archers leapt up at his command, peering out from the parapet with their bows at the ready.

Nunca released the first arrow; its three-pronged tail of eagle feathers whistling through the air before burying its twirling head into the neck of a charging warrior. At this signal, a thousand arrows were launched. Singing as they flew over the heads of the Northlanders, they blocked, for a heartbeat, the brilliance of the sun.

Volley upon volley rained upon Volger's troops and tempered the initial collision of opposing flesh and steel; for running men were halted in their tracks, dropping to the earth in their hundreds, as those following stumbled and tumbled upon bodies that began to litter the ground. But still that inevitable moment came, when superior numbers tipped the balance, and the deafening clash of hand to hand combat shattered the stillness of the day.

* * * * * *

"At last, *Sorcery for the Young Apprentice*," said Torpen gleefully, clutching the book to his chest; his eyes widening as the clamour of battle penetrated the chamber. "A Roun is what we need," he muttered.

"They say the elderly in their dotage regress to childhood. Well, if that be the case, perhaps I could perform some infantile sorcery." He chuckled nervously. "Sorcery that any half-witted child apprentice could do."

He laid the open book upon the floor of the eastern balcony, and bending forward stared at the words: repeating them over and over in his head. Ferneth fussed around him licking his face and nuzzling his ear. "Away my pet, there is sorcery to be done."

Straightening his back, Torpen closed his eyes and allowed the spell to form upon his lips which twitched into life as he silently mouthed the words. Turning northward, he opened his eyes and caught a glimpse of the river with its clear rushing waters glistening like a mighty jewel beneath the sun.

"Qualra Cumalaraith Cumalaraith Roun, Qualra Cumalaraith Cumalaraith Roun, Qualra Cumalaraith Cumalaraith Roun…" the old man chanted. He raised his arms towards the river; his fingers trembling as he closed his eyes and lifted his gaunt face to the sky. "Cumalaraith Roun, Cumalaraith Roun, Cumalaraith Roun."

Torpen opened one eye tentatively and glanced down towards the river. Rion, the giant stag, stood upon the bank drinking from the water. "Aah, Rion," he sighed despondently. "I did not call you, my friend, but it is always good to see you." His shoulders sank. "Perhaps I am too old…"

He turned his back and was about to step indoors when Rion raised his head, as a gentle mist began to stir upon the water; stretching his jaws wide he released a deep roar which echoed through the forest like a mighty clap of thunder. Torpen spun round.

"The Roun," he gasped with delight. "Come gentle friend. Come wrap your arms around Kinfallon. Come cool the air. Come cover the land. Come cloud the eyes of men."

* * * * * *

The Northlanders continued to hold their arc of ground, though the fighting proved ferocious. Zabian and Methna remained alongside those who defended the outer edges of the arc, ensuring, with the aid of Nunca's archers, that none of Volger's men were able to infiltrate the enclave from the rear. Aran and Jesyka, fighting side by side, continued to repel the onslaught that raged at the front.

The piles of crimson dead grew ever higher; hampering the advancement of thousands more who thrust eagerly forward in a desperate attempt to push through to the frontline. Shrill horns pierced the air above the clamour of battle, as Volger's men fell eerily quiet and began instantly to withdraw: dragging their dead and wounded with them.

Jesyka turned her back on the enemy. "They are clearing the plain of the dead," she yelled. "We must do likewise."

The Northlanders hurriedly began to move the bodies that lay upon the ground within the enclave. They banded together to drag or carry their dead and dying to rest upon the rubble at the rear. Flagons of water were hastily passed around, as many concentrated merely on breathing, dragging hungrily at the air, knowing that this unexpected moment of respite would soon be gone.

Jesyka stood beside Aran and watched as Volger's men loaded up carts with their dead; and then dragging them clear of the arc dumped them in piles to the east and the west.

Nunca signalled to his band of archers to descend the battlements. As they slithered down the rubble and leapt down into the Northland enclave, they were greeted with welcoming cheers from their weary countrymen.

"Your numbers are dropping," said Nunca to Zabian, as he slung his bow across his back and hauled the axes from their binding. "It is time we joined you."

Zabian raised his hand to rest upon Nunca's shoulder and smiled broadly. "It is hot work down here and the ground has softened." Nunca followed Zabian's gaze and they both stared down at his mud splattered boots.

Cupping his hands, Choi trilled like a bird, signalling to his archers to begin their descent. They slide down a plethora of ropes, which hung from the crenelated inner wall, and dropped to the earth within the spear-filled gully.

They eased their way through the tightly packed lances, crossing the terrain swiftly and clambering up the broken battlements to fill the landscape vacated by Nunca and his men.

Choi stood upon the wall, swept his arms upward like a bird about to take flight and stretched his fingers wide. Closing his eyes he breathed deeply. The Northlanders who accompanied him scrambled across the sprawling incline to crouch in silence amongst the debris and reload their bows.

As Choi began to rotate his wrists backwards and forwards, a gentle lift appeared at the corners of his mouth. He lowered his arms, allowing them to hang loose by his sides; as his fingers fluttered, their tips tapping softly against his thighs. Bending his elbows he raised his arms, palms upwards; before tucking his fingers beneath the edges of the scarlet sash where it crossed at the centre of his chest. Opening his cat-like eyes he allowed his gaze to fall upon the plain below as the fearsome cries of Volger's advancing warriors rose to meet him.

* * * * * *

Kamron's persistent biting at his lower lip eventually caused blood to flow: which he removed by repeatedly flicking his tongue across the broken skin.

"What nature of man is he?" asked Volger, leaning forward in the saddle to peer at Choi.

One of Volger's attendants stood in his stirrups and stared hard at the slight figure that raced to and fro across the broken stones. With a mere flick of the wrists, Choi released a seemingly endless supply of weaponry that flew through the air like a shower of shooting stars, before burying themselves deep into their fleshy targets.

"Further east, even than the desert lands," offered the attendant, "I have heard of an ancient race whose art of war is said to be as graceful as a dance."

Volger frowned; sucking savagely at the air. "Well, I have never seen his like before. He is laying waste to dozens."

"Our superior numbers will prevail, father, in the end," offered Kamron, pressing the back of his hand against his swollen lip. "They cannot hold out much longer."

"True enough, Kamron. Our task is almost complete." Volger exhaled deeply. "And yet to see our dead stand five times higher than that of the Northlanders does not please me. Any survivors will suffer richly for their impudence and their arrogance."

The attendant sat back in his saddle. "And yet it appears unlikely that there will be any survivors. They have given themselves no way of escape, and I doubt they will surrender. I would say it is their intention to fight to the death."

"Then so be it!" cried Volger, as he clenched his teeth.

Kamron swung round in his saddle to face his father. "But you did give instructions for the heir to be kept alive, father, did you not?"

Volger's jaw slackened. "Indeed, but in the heat of battle it is not always easy." He cleared his throat. "I have no doubt that the men will do their best."

"The men will do, father, what you command them to do. You gave me your word." Kamron's eye flickered and the blood oozed from his lip.

"What does it matter either way," snapped Volger, a sudden twitch of the head registering his annoyance. "If the guardians, the heir and Lord Aran die then we will have accomplished everything. We have no need of the heir now – she is surplus to requirements."

"My Lords," hissed the attendant. "I fear we have a more pressing problem." Volger and Kamron followed the attendant's gaze to the brow of the hill directly above them. "Wolves, my Lords."

Kyler and Akir stood side by side upon the summit. Throwing back their heads in unison, they delivered a shrill, menacing howl.

"We must flee, my Lords," cried the attendant. "There is no time to lose."

Volger sniggered. "From two wolves, I think not."

"Not two, my Lord, more like a hundred and two."

Wolves began to gather as new arrivals squeezed their slender bodies between those already present until they stood shoulder to shoulder across the western horizon. A hooded man upon horseback appeared amongst them; his head bent forward as he surveyed the battle below, until, in his peripheral vision, he caught sight of the small party within the copse. He grinned, raised his head and swept the hood from his sandy coloured hair.

"The Eastlander," cried Kamron, as his face contorted, flushing violently.

"Follow me, my Lords," cried the attendant; launching his horse headlong down the hillside.

Volger, Kamron and the remaining attendants, frantically spurred their mounts into action as they followed close upon his heels. The riders, making no attempt to restrain the momentum of the sprinting horses, ploughed indiscriminately into the vast column of marching men. Driving relentlessly forward, the horsemen pushed on until they disappeared from view, swallowed by the swaying throng.

Balac lifted his eyes from the milieu and watched as dark shapes began to emerge from the forest on the eastern side of the plain. He raised a hand, shielding his squinting eyes from the brightness of the day.

"Dear God," he muttered, shaking his head. "If I had not seen it with my own eyes…" He allowed his head to fall back and roared with laughter. "More four-legged recruits, my beauties," he called.

Rion was the first to step from the trees. He strode majestically, with his head held high, as he led an immense herd of red deer out onto the plain.

Choi cupped his hands and delivered an uncanny ear-piercing cry that he knew the guardians would hear: even above the din of the battle. Nunca was the first to swing round as Choi gestured to the west and then to the east. Nunca lifted his eyes to stare above the chaos and smiled; raising his axe aloft he confirmed to Choi that he had seen all.

"*Balac*," screamed Jesyka, thrusting her broadsword high into the air and staring wide-eyed at the vision upon the hillside. "*Balac*," she screamed again.

"Ah, so that is the mystery wolf man," said Methna as she appeared at Jesyka's side. "And Rion too. Look, he stands to the east."

"Dear God," gasped Jesyka. "Whatever next?"

"You may well ask, for Choi has sent word, there is a Roun rising from the river and heading this way. Within minutes this battlefield will disappear." Methna grabbed at Jesyka's elbow and swung her round to face her. "Jesyka, you and Aran must go with Zabian and head for the forest while there is still time."

Jesyka shook her head, trying to focus upon her mother's words. "A Roun?"

"Yes, fantastical though it seems. Choi believes it may be Torpen's doing. He is trying to give us a chance, a chance to live. And you and Aran must take it…"

"But we cannot abandon all who have stood beside us all who have given so much," cried out Jesyka.

"Choi is the only one who can lead the Northlanders to safety through the Roun and he is preparing to do so now.

But you must flee." Methna glanced back over her shoulder as the gentle rolling mist appeared upon the battlements. "See," she cried, stabbing at the air with an outstretched arm. "Here it comes."

Jesyka swallowed hard and sheathed her sword.

"Come Jesyka," yelled Zabian. "We must head for the trees. We must not squander this gift – for against all the odds – that crazy, wonderful old man has offered us a way out."

"Mother, will you not come with us?" called Jesyka.

Methna nodded towards the west. "I think the man who gave me back my daughter also deserves a chance to live." She smiled and reaching forward brushed away a smear of blood from Jesyka's cheek. "No heroics, I promise." And with that Methna turned upon her heels and was gone.

"Come, Jesyka," said Zabian, "we can wait no longer."

"What of Nunca?" she asked.

"I have no doubt he will be doing what he always does – which is aiding, as well as annoying, his little friend," replied Zabian with a grin.

As she felt Aran's blood-stained hand heavy upon her shoulder, she lifted moist eyes to stare into his weary face.

As the damp cool air of the Roun lurched after them, they ran headlong towards the trees. The sun was beginning to fade; its heat and light diluted by the rising mist. Under the mutating light, the vibrant purples and greens of the early spring landscape grew grey and still.

Balac flung back his cloak, drew the sword from the scabbard at his waist, and urged his horse to charge down the hillside. The wolves shot forward in pursuit, quickly gathering about Balac, as they swept like a great dark shadow across the land.

Rion bent his head and shook his mighty antlers. Pawing at the ground, a roar began to rumble within his throat as he leapt forward with astonishing speed. The herd followed him, thundering out across the softening earth, throwing up clumps of limp grass and mud, as they bore down upon Volger's men on the eastern flank.

37

The Roun stole silently around the base of the castle, its tentacles swirling upwards. It began to slither through the trees and creep up the craggy abyss to trickle across the narrow roadway and down towards the plain.

"Sorcery is abound!" yelled Volger, spittle bubbling at the corners of his gaping mouth. "First the wild beasts of the forest and now this…" he spluttered. "What is this damnable fog?"

"Tis a Roun, my Lord," said the attendant. "It rolls in off the water sometimes. But not on a day such as this." The man stared up at the castle which was beginning to grow hazy and shivered in the damp air.

"There, my Lord, the old man at the window. He is dressed in sorcerer's robes."

Torpen's tall thin frame shook, as he roared with jubilant laughter and tears of joy coursed his parched cheeks.

"Someone take him down!" screamed Volger. "We must put a halt to this accursed Roun." He grabbed at the attendant's arm. "Ride forward and fell the sorcerer before we are all lost in this infernal fog."

The arrow entered Torpen's chest with such force that it threw him back to land upon the chaotic table: scattering books and potions to crash and splatter upon the floor. Ferneth released an agonising cry and leapt up. She crouched at his feet and then inched her way up the old man's prostrate body, until she lay, with her head upon his chest beside the fateful arrow. Torpen smiled weakly, and raised a hand to lay upon the trembling ebony coat.

"Well, well, Ferneth," he whispered; as his eyes fluttered shut. "There was still some life in the old dog, eh?"

* * * * * *

The deafening clash and roar of battle began to subside, as the Roun gathered speed and billowed out across the plain. Then the voices, many voices, began to cry out, calling the names of those known to them; as they attempted to locate someone, anyone, in the sightless world of the Roun.

Methna ran straight for the heather-strewn hillside which was fading quickly before her eyes. She sensed movement all around her as people scrambled along the ground feeling their way; someone banged against her leg and she swung round, grabbing at the dagger at her waist, but they were gone in an instant. It was impossible to distinguish friend from foe in the thickening fog as the air cooled rapidly and the battlefield grew strangely quiet. She forced her eyes wider and stared straight ahead.

Methna's foot hit against the bottom of the hill, and with a relieved sigh, she began to scramble upwards. Her breathing became laboured as she sucked at the damp air, determined to rise above the mist before it swallowed the hillside completely. When she burst through the dense white blanket, heat and light enveloped her as she stood once more in the brilliant sunshine. Turning south she could see the dozen trees which made up the small copse just beneath the summit: the point where Balac had charged towards the plain.

Stopping just below the copse she could hear beneath her the snapping and snarling of wolves and the piteous cries of men.

"Balac!" she yelled, cupping her hands about her mouth in an effort to direct her words down into the haze. "Balac, save yourself. Jesyka lives. She is safe."

Methna waited as the Roun continued to rise and lap around her feet.

"Jesyka lives, Balac. There is no more to be done. The day is lost. Save yourself," she cried once more.

Kamron sat astride his horse which was wandering aimlessly about the battlefield. He detected the odd muffled voice calling in the distance and the occasional shuffling sound as someone passed close-by; but could see nothing and made no attempt to steer his horse in any particular direction. And then he heard Methna's cry.

At first he could not make out the actual words but taking up the reins began to move towards the voice. And then it came again and this time he heard: "Jesyka lives…" He lowered his head and his shoulders heaved, as a great sigh of relief burst from him. Lifting his head he allowed it to roll backwards until his neck grew taut.

"She lives," he whispered, towards the unseen sky. "She lives…" A wide grin, followed by a snort of laughter was quickly replaced by a sneer, as he turned his horse and began to move away from the voice. "That's all I needed to know," he murmured.

As Methna stood peering down into the mist, Akir leapt out of the whiteness. Crouching low she lifted her snout, bared strong gleaming teeth and uttered a soft curdling growl. Blood pulsed from a ragged tear above her right ear and she blinked as it trickled down into her eye. Methna met Akir's stare and dropping to her knees, lifted her hand slowly and held it out towards her. Akir's nostrils dilated as she drew hard at the air; straightening her legs she rose graciously to her full height, threw back her head and released a short shrill howl.

And then they came; emerging from the mist: Balac and a host of wolves.

His damp hair lay sprawled about his shoulders and his green eyes blazed.

"She is safe?"

"Yes, she is already on her way to the coast," said Methna.

A gentle smile spread across Balac's face.

"Will you come with me, Balac? I can lead you to safety. But we must go now for the Roun is still rising."

Without hesitation he dropped to his knees and turned to face the pack that closed in around him. Reaching forward, he cradled first Kyler's and then Akir's face within his hands. Akir flashed her rough hot tongue across his face and whimpered.

"All is well, my friends. We have done enough. And now it is time for you to go home," said Balac, pushing his fingers through the soft mud-splattered fur at Akir's throat. "And time for me to move on."

As the Roun swirled up around them, he rose to his feet. "Take care of one another."

He stepped away, and then turning back suddenly, bent forward and gently brushed the blood away from Akir's eye with his thumb. "Hey, and don't nag the old man too much. Remember he's getting on a bit."

Raising his eyes to the horizon, where Methna stood waiting, he gestured with a nod that he would follow; as Akir and Kyler, moving silently away, led the pack south towards the Eastland.

* * * * * *

Jesyka, realising she was some way ahead of Zabian and Aran, slowed her pace to a steady walk.

She thought she could hear someone calling, way in the distance. Or was it just in her head? She could not be sure.

"Run, Jesyka, run," cried the voice.

As she stopped and pressed her back against the trunk of a towering pine, she felt consumed by the pain that pulsed through every fibre and muscle of her body. She winced as she raised her left hand to press at the throbbing muscles across her right shoulder, and then changed hands to squeeze at the muscles in her left. She was battle weary and needed to sleep. She closed her eyes.

And then the voice came again. "Live, Jesyka, live."

"Father?" she whispered.

She must survive she knew that; she owed it to that huge sacrifice of life that lay scattered upon the plain. The Roun had given the Northlanders a last gasp at life. They had done all they could, been prepared to give everything, and then in the final throes of the battle, Balac had come and Rion too... so much giving, so much loss. She swallowed hard, forcing back the tears.

"Live, Jesyka, live," came the voice again.

"Yes, father," she whispered in response; as a great swell rose in her breast. "Yes, I understand," she nodded gently.

She heard footsteps approaching and opened her eyes. Aran, grim-faced and breathing heavily came to a halt before her and fell to his knees. Zabian, moving at a constant easy pace, ran straight past.

Jesyka gave a short weary laugh.

"Why is he not stopping?" gasped Aran.

"Because he knows, that if you stop, you will feel the pain more acutely," she grinned.

"Aaah," groaned Aran, as he struggled to stand. "Is he right about everything?"

"Just about," she replied.

Aran stood swaying, a deep frown set above pleading eyes. "This is agony. How much further must we run?"

Jesyka stepped towards him and planted a gentle kiss upon his cheek.

"Can you smell the salt air?" she asked. "We are almost there. No more than a mile."

"A mile," he groaned, rolling his eyes heavenward in dismay.

"Actually, it's probably more like two."

She smiled broadly, as he grasped her proffered hand, and together they followed Zabian towards the coast and the smell of the sea.

* * * * * *

High above the rolling Roun, Sirus, the silver-backed eagle, soared with wings outstretched; the edges of his feathers lifted in the light breeze and shimmered beneath the glare of the sun. Circling above the billowing mist he cried out to the still, silent earth below.

At last his patience was rewarded, for the weathervane that stood atop the highest tower of Kinfallon Castle, pierced the white shroud, as the Roun began its retreat. Sirus continued to hover over the scene, until the roof of the tower loomed large through the haze. Folding back his mighty wings and reaching out with talons spread wide, he finally came to rest upon the tower.

Rapidly curling and swirling away into nothingness, the thinning fog was punctured by shafts of golden light, as the sun reconnected with the land. The devastation that lay sprawled across the plain consisted of both men and beasts. Broken bodies and weapons lay intertwined; the twisted and pierced flesh that could no longer see or feel the light and the heat of the day lay like some odious tapestry upon the land.

Sirus took flight once more; circling for the last time above Kinfallon, he released a torturous scream that rang out across the Northland: beyond the hills to the west and the tall trees to the east. Then, with a few steady beats of his wings, he climbed high above the earth, set his head to the south and began his journey home; for the siege of the Northland was over and the day was lost.

Epilogue

As the arrow entered Torpen's heart, Daracha inhaled sharply and stopped. She had been queuing to board the *Escabar*: by far the largest sea vessel she had ever seen. She thrust a hand deep into her coat pocket and toyed with the two gold coins which lay at the bottom: the cost of passage to a new life.

"Hey, move along there lassie. Come on, we don't have all day," called a voice from behind. She made as if to step forward, but found to her surprise that some unknown force appeared to pull her to the side.

"Torpen," she murmured under her breath, "you old devil."

Bodies surged forward, quickly filling the gap, as the snake of people shuffled along and Daracha absentmindedly stood and waited. Eventually she stopped playing with the coins and abandoned them to the murky depths of the pocket: smiling as she heard then chink together at the bottom.

As the mist continued to thicken and hover over the harbour, she turned up the heavy woollen collar of her old patchwork coat; the moisture gathering on her tightly curled black hair and over-long lashes.

"There won't be another passenger-ship leaving the Southland for over a month, dearie," said an elderly woman, with warm crinkly eyes. "You can step back in next to me," she offered, gesturing towards Daracha. "I'd enjoy the company."

"Thank you, but no," she replied, turning her large brown eyes to meet the woman's expectant face. "I forgot, it seems that an old friend is calling in a favour," she smiled broadly.

"Then God be with you child," replied the old woman; drawing a threadbare hood over her long white hair as she ambled away.

"I hope so," said Daracha, turning from the crowd, as she contemplated the long trek north.

* * * * * *

It was dusk when a man in a long dark coat, and boots caked in mud, strode along the rain-lashed harbour. From beneath a furrowed brow his dark eyes flitted across the bay, as a quickening wind caused the ships at berth to wrestle with their moorings. He stopped by a swinging lantern hanging from the stern of the *Dancing Monkey* and, glancing down, noted that the rain had relieved his boots of much of the mud. He walked swiftly up the gangplank and disappeared below deck.

A single candle lit the cabin where Captain Quiggs sat at the table, considering the open bottle of rum and the three full glasses which sat in the centre. He glanced down as the door creaked open and smiled as he beheld the boots and their owner. Zabian bent his head and stepped through the doorway. Returning to his full height he eased out his shoulders, unfastened the dripping coat and with a sigh lowered himself into the seat opposite the Captain.

"So Captain, are all your passengers abed?" asked Zabian, fixing his eyes upon the rum.

"All but one," Captain Quiggs replied, with a furtive nod towards the corner of the room, "someone very keen to make your acquaintance." He paused. "And pick your brains about the desert lands."

Zabian raised an eyebrow quizzically and narrowing his eyes peered into the darkness. A body shifted upon the narrow bench and leant forward into the small circle of light that surrounded the flickering candle.

"Ah," said Zabian, with a wistful smile, as Balac raised heavy eyelids and met his inquisitive gaze. "You are most welcome, my friend."

Only the sound of straining timbers accompanied the three men, as they raised their glasses in unison and drank.